MW01180959

Also by Marcia Canter **Every Woman's Tale** and **Mosquito Madness.**

For more information on Marcia's books, go to Booklanthropy.com.

A Different Kind of Christmas and Other Stories

Marcia Canter

ISBN: 978-1-4834-2209-1 (sc)
ISBN: 978-1-4834-2208-4 (e)

Lulu Publishing Services rev. date: 10/6/2015

Dedication

To my family who have always made Christmas a
wonderful time in my life as well as giving me joy,
love, support, and laughter the rest of the year.

Contents

Preface

I come from a family of storytellers as well as people who make a difference in other people's lives. When I decided to publish these stories and my other works, I not only wanted to entertain the reader but I wanted to continue making a difference. I've established an organization called Booklanthropy whose goal is to use reading to help others. To learn more about my other works and causes, go to Booklanthropy.com. A portion of my books' revenues will support these causes. **A Different Kind of Christmas and Other Stories** will support groups assisting veterans and their families.

Acknowledgements

The list of people I have to thank is about as long as Santa's toy list. First there is my editor, Kate R. Canter, who gave me ideas to expand the stories and smoothed out the rough spots. Clayhill Creative LLC designed my cover. My brother, Roger, gave me my first memorable Christmas when we woke up at 4 a.m. to play with the bowling pin set under the tree. Later he helped me with the review of the stories, sharing his male perspective. My sister, Ruth, told me lots of stories when we were growing up, and read this book with the eye of a teacher who had corrected papers for thirty years. My daughter, Anne, as well as other friends and other family members, read the stories and encouraged me. (Any grammatical or writing errors, however, are my own gifts to encourage people not to be perfect.) My husband, Bob, has been with me the last thirty-eight Christmases and all the days in between. As Tiny Tim would say "God bless us every one."

The Dancer

Christmas without going to the Nutcracker Ballet would be like skipping the tree for me. Even when I am up to my eyeballs in shopping, parties, and juggling work with the 101 things on my to-do-list, I make time for it. It's not the music or the dancing but the memory of my friend Paula, a young girl named Elizabeth, and Elizabeth's mother that keeps me going year after year.

Paula Collins was my savior my first year of teaching. She had sixteen years of teaching kindergartners by the time I arrived at Sloan's Elementary, fresh out of college. Each morning every child received Paula's one of a kind smiles, a smile that said: "You are so special. You matter to me." She could walk into a classroom of kids running around, hold her hand up, silently mouth the words one, two, three, and by four they'd be seated and quiet.

She had her lesson plans down pat. If it was the 20th week of school, it was time to do the '100 project' when the kids brought in samples of something adding up to 100. Her walls were lined with toothpick stars, Tootsie roll wreathes, and pennies, lots of pennies. Paula counted every button and penny to make sure the project was perfect. She was the perfect teacher and I couldn't stand her at first.

Funny how someone's strengths tend to make your weaknesses show up that much more. Paula didn't mean to outshine me. All she ever tried to do was give those twenty-four kindergartners the best start she could toward academic success. I, on the other hand, could only try to get through each day at a time without throwing something at my third graders. Sometimes it was hour by hour; sometimes minute by minute.

She would stop by after school when I would be sitting at my desk without any voice left, and softly say, smiling her Paula smile, "Maybe if you talk quieter, they'll have to listen to you." I tried it and it worked. Some of the time.

One day, after a particularly embarrassing meltdown the day before, she brought in cupcakes for my class. "Tell them that each student who doesn't get his or her name written up today will get a cupcake." Everyone got a cupcake that day.

She was perfect. Her room was perfect too--a magical delight for any five-year-old coming to school. Pictures of dragons, vibrant colored words on the wall, number games everywhere. She also had a picture of every child hung up on the wall with a complement that she wrote underneath. On her own desk, her family portrait displayed a husband with a full head of greying hair, a tall teenaged girl with her mother's dusty colored hair pulled back into a ponytail and Paula, beaming with the radiance of someone who couldn't be happier.

Paula's radiance went out on a Tuesday morning in November. As I crossed the playground in semi-darkness, I saw a little pink backpack lying by the swings. Inside was the kindergartner folder. I smiled. For once I could do something nice for Paula or at least one of her students.

The school was still quiet when I came down the hall, but I could hear voices coming out of the kindergarten room. I walked in to see Principal Hamilton giving Paula a big hug.

They looked up with tears streaming down their faces. "I am sorry," I mumbled heading for the door.

"No, Lissa, don't be," Paula said. "I was just telling Sophia some of my problems."

"Now you don't have to be here, honey," the principal's Southern roots showed as she put her arm around Paula.

"God, I do…I can't be at the house." She breathed in deeply, her frame shaking with emotion.

"Why, what happened?" I couldn't help asking, wondering if there had been a fire or a break-in.

"Karlie," she choked out. "Karlie, my daughter tried, committing suicide last night. We found her just in time."

"Oh, I am so sorry." I didn't know what else to say.

"I just can't believe it," she went on in a rapid staccato voice so different than the normal, calm sounding voice. "I never saw it coming. It's all my fault. Bob thinks we pushed her too hard. And she broke up with Kevin last month. I thought she was just pulling away from some of her friends, too hard to be there. I never knew. I knew she lost weight, but damn it, isn't that what we're always doing?" After that flood of words, she collapsed back in Hamilton's arms.

"Honey, let's get a sub today." Hamilton rubbed her shoulders. Paula shook her head.

"No," her voice rang out clearly. "I will be here. I will be ok. Lissa," she said, taking a long, deep breath. "I know you're not a gossipy type, but right now I can't stand to have anyone else know about this. I can't talk about it." I nodded. Hamilton threw me a look that told me if I broke the confidence, I would be on lunch duty the rest of the year.

Paula smiled back bleakly and then mouthed "Thank you. Then she took another deep breath, steadier this time, and stood up

"Well, I better get the reading books ready for today's book bags. Excuse me, ladies," and she went to the reading center and started matching kids with books they hadn't read.

"Show me your lesson plan for today," Hamilton ordered loudly as she escorted me out of the hall.

We went to my classroom, and I immediately started rummaging through my satchel.

"I don't want to see your lesson plan, Miss Foley," she whispered, the way a drill sergeant might whisper commands, "but I didn't want Paula to know about this discussion. I am assigning you to her. I want you to go over at lunch and ask her help on something, just so that she can keep busy for a while. I am sure there's something you can use help with," she said looking at my cluttered desk. I agreed quickly. The first year of teaching kills foolish pride.

When I walked in right after her morning kids had left for the day, Paula was just staring at her family picture, tears rolling down her face. "Paula," I said without looking at the picture because I was afraid I might cry, "would you help me with a lesson plan I am trying to do for Thanksgiving? Can you come over and see what I've got?"

She walked in and immediately went over to the messiest desk in the classroom. "Whose desk is this?" she asked in a disgusted voice.

"Danny Rodriquez."

"Oh, I had him as a kindergartner," Paula smiled slightly. "He has some spatial problems. You need to make him clean this mess up or he won't find anything. Who's next to him?"

"Charlie Clarke."

"Get them apart," Paula advised. "They will talk too much and Danny can't handle that much distraction. Then you won't be trying to police them all the time."

"I could put Demi Keller between them," I said thinking of my star girl.

"I like Demi," she said softly with a break in her voice. "She loves to run, just like Karlie."

I swallowed. "Why don't you tell me about Karlie?"

Paula seemed to need to collect all her feelings together before she could speak. "She was perfect, an excellent student and athlete. Last year she placed fifth at state cross country."

"I ran cross country."

The woman went on without paying any attention to my admission. "Karlie blew out her knee this year and couldn't compete. I am so damn blind…I didn't see all the things that happened to her this year."

"Paula," I tried to come up with the right words. "You did the best you could. I am sure of that."

"Then tell me why my daughter is in a psychiatric ward," she said looking straight at me "instead of English class." With that, she marched out of the room, never asking about what help I needed for my Thanksgiving lesson plan.

But when the bell rang, I heard her call her afternoon class to attention the same way she did every day.

Hamilton checked on both of us a lot that afternoon. At dismissal she was at the exit by our rooms. "Well?" she whispered while Paula talked to a couple of mothers.

I shrugged. "She's coping. She's doing remarkably well."

Paula stopped in my room that afternoon at three-thirty. "I wanted to tell you thanks…"

I waved my hand. "Go see your daughter." She smiled and walked out quickly.

She was back the next morning, looking extremely tired. "How's it going?" I asked cautiously.

"I don't know. I don't have the answers. Karlie is mad at us for talking to her friends and teachers. She can barely look at us." She closed her eyes and for the first time I could see the lines of care and age that her positivity usually erased.

"Maybe she's embarrassed."

"Or pissed," Paula's bluntness surprised me. "But I guess that's an improvement over dead. Let me look at those individualized lesson plans. I can tell you what I would do for those kids I had."

She returned at noon. We were sitting together at my desk looking over the portfolio of one when Margie Harper, the fifth-grade teacher, waltzed in.

"There you are," she said to Paula, holding an envelope in her hand. "I've got something for you."

"What's that?" Paula had no smile for Margie.

"Elizabeth Walker brought this in for you, but you were in a meeting so I said I'd give it to you."

Paula opened the envelope and quickly scanned the contents. "Oh no," she grimaced and covered her face with her hands. I swallowed, wondering what further tragedy had been heaped on this poor woman.

"What is it?" Margie said.

"Oh," she sighed, "tickets to the Nutcracker Ballet. Elizabeth is one of the sugarplums this year. She's invited me to come to opening night."

"Really? Who doesn't like the Nutcracker Ballet and gobs of little girls all dressed up?" Margie asked incredulously.

"No, I do. It's just that Karlie's been sick and I guess I'm overwhelmed."

"Don't worry. High school girls always get sick," Margie said. "I better check my lunch before someone swipes it out of the refrigerator."

"Oh," Paula said, watching her flounce out of my classroom. "Now she and everybody will wonder what's going on at my house. But I just can't think about going right now."

"Just tell Elizabeth no," I suggested.

"It's not that easy," she went on. "It would mean a lot to Elizabeth for me to come. Do you know her?"

There were 400 kids in the school and I still struggled sometimes remembering my own twenty students' names. I shook my head.

"I've had almost 300 students since I started teaching here," Paula said. "Every one is different and yet every one is almost the same. Elizabeth Walker was someone that caught my attention from day one and has held it ever since. Beautiful girl, tall, thin, with long dark hair either tied back or in a bun. The first morning she came in with her grandmother, Helen Rogers. Helen was not like the other grandmothers we see but a very frail yet elegant lady. Elizabeth was so quiet and so different than the other kids. It was like she was in mourning, but she was smart and didn't cause me any trouble so I didn't worry too much about her.

"It wasn't until conferences that I met Elizabeth's mother, Karen, for the first time. Helen came too, of course. Karen was on one of those motorized wheelchairs. We weren't really very equipped for that so I guess they had to go through the back entrance by the gym to get in. Karen was all red-faced from having the janitors having to help her." Paula then smiled.

"But that night Elizabeth was a different kid. She beamed that night with lots of giggling and talking above a whisper. I had never seen her so happy.

"Her mother just nodded and smiled and stroked her daughter's hair without saying a word. The two were almost identical in their beauty. When we sat down at conferences, I wasn't sure what to do, whether to talk to the grandmother or the mother about how Elizabeth was doing. I guessed I talked to both of them. But Karen said nothing the whole time.

"'Does she have any friends?' the grandmother asked when I finished talking to them about Elizabeth's strengths.

"'Not any close ones.' I had to be honest even though the child was right there. 'I don't think they dislike her. I think she just doesn't get close to them.'

"'Oh, honey, why is that?' her grandmother asked and Karen's eyes teared up.

'I don't know,' Elizabeth said simply. 'They're nice, but they seem like babies.'

"As they were leaving, I saw the grandmother look at her daughter and Karen jerk her head just a little. The granddaughter and grandmother left the room. I'll never forget the first words Karen Walker spoke to me.

"'I….' she seemed to be looking for words, 'need….help.'

"I told her I would help her anyway I could. I had no idea what was coming.

"'I want to be' ….and she searched for words again. 'A good…. mother.'

"I said something lame like we all want to be good mothers and with that she nodded and wheeled off. Helen came back after school the next day. 'Did Karen ask you for help?' she asked after we exchanged pleasantries.

"I nodded. 'But I don't know if I understand what she wants. She said she wants to be a good mother. I'm confused to why she's talking to me. You seem to be there and helping her a lot.

"'But not forever.' The lady looked me straight in the eye. 'I'm dying.'"

Paula gulped as if she had been given the news again. The bell rang. It made both of us jump but saved me from having to think of something to say. "I've got to meet my kids," Paula said as she rushed off, dabbing her eyes.

Hamilton met me at my door when the kids were coming in. "What did you say to Paula?" she hissed. "She looked as if she was going to cry. Did you upset her?"

"No," I said. "She was telling me about a girl named Elizabeth whose mother was in a wheelchair."

"Elizabeth Walker. Yes, that's a great idea. Talk to her more after school."

The thought of raising this sorrow up again for Paula chilled me the rest of the afternoon. But the thought of having to face Hamilton was even worse.

I poked my head into Paula's room after the kids were let out of school.

"Paula, what happened to Elizabeth and her mother?"

"What do you mean? They are here."

"I mean, how did they manage? I have been wondering what happened all afternoon. The girl is still here."

Paula smiled. "That was pretty amazing. When Elizabeth's grandmother told me that she was dying, all I could say was so stupid like how sorry I was. Without missing a beat, Helen told me she was worried about Karen losing custody of Elizabeth and she wanted me to make sure Karen would be able to oversee Elizabeth's schooling. She explained how Karen and her husband, Charlie, were in a terrible car accident. Charlie was killed instantly, and Karen hit her head hard. She has permanent brain damage. Little Elizabeth was in her car seat in the back and came out of it without a scratch.

"I remember how Helen laughed bitterly that day. 'She wasn't hurt in the least unless you count the fact that her daddy was killed and her mother is not the same.'

"Helen's husband was dead so she just moved in with them. They bought a house and fixed it so that Karen could move around easily. Things were going along well until Helen's doctor told her she had only six months to live.

'It would kill Karen to lose her daughter,' the woman told me, bypassing the fact that her mother and caregiver was about to die.

"I asked her what I could do, as calmly as I could, but the seriousness of what was to come had me shaking.

'I want you to help Karen to be able to help her daughter with homework and to fit into school. Elizabeth is very smart, but Karen doesn't remember her multiplication tables anymore. Karen is relearning how to write her name. Reading is difficult for her.'

"Despite her cognitive challenges, even Karen was aware that the school had the obligation to report any evidence that Elizabeth was being neglected. 'I want you to make sure that she isn't neglected as far as you can tell. Karen won't do anything intentionally, but I don't know what she needs to know.'

Paula smiled and sighed at the same time. "So our history together began. I would call Karen up in the afternoon and tell her what Elizabeth needed to do that night. Karen sometimes came in at noon to work on the exercises and reading so that she would know what the story was about. She practiced every single letter with Elizabeth. Elizabeth's penmanship was better than Karen's, but Karen kept working at it. Karen worked hard at everything she tried— from penmanship to making lunches to carrying on conversations over the phone.

"The doctor was overly optimistic," Paula said looking down. "By Thanksgiving Helen was bedridden. Her cancer had gone so fast. But Karen now could pack Elizabeth a lunch every day. She was safe using the stove, and Helen had set up the bank account to automatically pay the mortgage, the electricity, the water bill."

She smiled her normal Paula smile for the first time since she started telling the story. "Then after Thanksgiving our class got a special surprise. A business donated tickets for us to go to the Nutcracker Ballet. I sent home a note saying that I needed volunteers to chaperone. The first response was written in little capital letters saying that Karen was willing to go. She wanted to go.

"I wrote her back a note thanking her but asked if she thought she would be able to manage in the wheelchair. The next morning she walked Elizabeth to school using crutches. Karen came down to my room, madder than hell.

'I can manage,' she said, hardly stuttering. 'I will come on this field trip.'

"And she did. Of course the kids were curious about what had happened to Karen. But Elizabeth answered all the questions calmly with pride. She told them how her mom was in a bad accident and hit her head and that made her not able to walk very well or to talk quickly.

"The kids were ok with Karen after that. Some were restless during the performance, but Karen and Elizabeth were mesmerized by it all. When they came out, their cheeks were glowing and their eyes bright.

"Elizabeth waited until everyone was sitting on the bus, and then she pulled out a picture in a gold frame. 'Look, here's my mom. She was Clara.'

"The little girls oohed as they looked at the beautiful Karen in a white night gown, standing perfectly on pointe. Elizabeth looked just like the girl in the photograph.

"Helen called and invited me over the next afternoon. Karen and Elizabeth were listening to the music from the Nutcracker. There was one thing more for me to do—find someone to take Elizabeth to ballet lessons, just the way her mother had. Like the electricity and water bill, Helen had put money aside for that.

"That was the last time I saw Helen. She died over Christmas break. I went to the funeral and then told Karen what her mother asked."

Paula's eyes were now shiny again with tears. "I found a high school girl who wanted to take lessons. Her parents take them both. It's been five years since she started, and now Elizabeth is one of the sugarplums this year. She's worked hard and her instructor tells me that she may be Clara someday. Karen has worked hard too, but sometimes gets terribly depressed, and talks of maybe giving Elizabeth up."

Paula sighed. "I used to go over about every week and talk to them. But then we became so busy with our own lives, and Elizabeth seemed to be doing so well. Karen comes in and sees me when she is at school, and she always asks how Karlie is doing. Karlie babysat for Elizabeth a couple of years when Karen and I went Christmas shopping. Elizabeth loves Karlie." Her voice broke. "I don't think I can explain. I don't think I can tell her."

Once again there was nothing I could think of to say. There was nothing to say. Paula seemed to forget I was in the room. She stared for a time at her family picture. Then she put it down. "She thinks about giving up her baby, and I'm worried that I've lost mine," she said as she walked out of the room.

I went back to my room but just sat at my desk for a long time after that. Eventually, when the janitor began to pointedly vacuum around me, I forced myself to get up and go home. Everything felt so far away after listening to Paula's story, knowing what I knew about the Walker family and Paula's daughter. Karlie had put herself in a hospital while another little girl practiced ballet. Two mothers worked so hard, going above and beyond the call of duty, to have such different outcomes for their children. I barely slept that night and staggered into work with no more answers than I started with.

When Paula came into my room the next day, she was smiling her Paula smile again. "I have an extra ticket to the Nutcracker Suite," she said, presenting them to me over my coffee. "Bob is out of town that night. Lissa, would you come with me?"

"I thought you couldn't leave Karlie."

"I thought about it. I guess I decided that I needed to go. Karen and Elizabeth were looking forward to me being there. I decided that I would tell Karlie that I couldn't be there that night."

"And you know what?" Paula grinned. "She said 'Good! Now maybe you're not going to worry about me all the time.' It was ok. She wanted me to go. I know Karlie is safe at the hospital. I really want to go, Lissa. Would you come with me?"

The opening night was the day after Thanksgiving. Paula picked me up at my apartment promptly at six. "We're to meet them there after the performance. The parents sit in a special section."

It was a gala event with women in long dresses and men in tuxedos. We could see the parent section but couldn't spot Karen. "I should have picked her up, but she said she had a way of getting there," Paula said guiltily, but then the ballet started.

"There's Elizabeth," Paula whispered, pointing to the young girl leading the sugar plum fairies' procession. I don't know anything about ballet, but I wished I had the presence that Elizabeth and the other dancers showed. The night went quickly and of course there were standing ovations. Then the crowds thinned out.

"They take pictures of the girls afterwards. Let's get closer," Paula said, as we put on our coats.

As we started down the aisle, we saw a woman in a long black dress, walk slowly with a small limp, carrying a bouquet of roses, up the stairs and across the stage. Elizabeth broke away from the group and ran to her mother who was not using crutches. Paula was crying as we made our way to the stage. When we reached the stage, Elizabeth bounded over and gave Paula a rose. The woman with the limp followed her daughter.

"You were wonderful," Paula said. I didn't know if she was talking to Elizabeth or Karen or both.

"We couldn't have done it," Karen stuttered, "without you."

"Let's go have some coffee to celebrate," Paula said after introductions were made. "How did you get here?" she asked Karen.

Karen smiled and her eyes showed her confidence. "I took the bus. I went shopping too."

"Without crutches," Elizabeth spoke with pride.

The women and the dancer hugged again. "You are both beautiful tonight. I can't believe it," Paula said when she finally pulled away.

"Let me take your picture together," I offered.

The smiles on their face could have lit up that stage. It was the first time since Karlie's suicide attempt that Paula seemed totally herself. When we left, we walked across the parking lot, arms looped together.

To celebrate, we stopped for coffee and cheesecake. Karen ate very slowly, but surely. "How do you like... Sloan's?" she said suddenly.

"I like it. The kids are wonderful and the staff is great."

"Especially Mrs. Collins," she added.

"Especially Mrs. Collins," I agreed. "I'm very lucky to have her across the hall from me."

"So what are you doing," Karen asked Paula, "for Christmas? Going skiing?"

"I don't know," Paula said. "Karlie hasn't been well this fall."

"Oh," Karen's face clouded up. "I'm sorry. We miss her."

"I'll tell her that. She'll want to see you sometime, maybe over Christmas. Elizabeth, what do you want for Christmas?"

"Books," she answered and then smiled, "and maybe a computer."

"Oh, I don't know much about computers, but Lissa does," Paula said, smiling at me.

"Would you...." Karen hesitated, maybe because of her disability, maybe shyness..."would you help us?"

"I'd love to," I told her. "We could go tomorrow if you want."

Elizabeth grinned. "Cool. That would be so cool."

"Go early?" Karen asked. "Beat the crowds?"

"Sure, I go running early. Right after that."

We finished our celebration, and Paula insisted on driving them home. The mother and daughter were slowly going up to the house when Elizabeth tugged on her mother's sleeve. They whispered, and then Elizabeth came back running to our car.

"Here Ms. Foley, take one of my roses. To remember tonight. We'll see you in the morning." She ran back to her mother.

We drove to my apartment in silence. "Don't forget your rose," Paula said as I started to get out.

I shook my head. "Take this to Karlie. Tell her that Elizabeth missed her and wanted her to have it. Then tell her how far they've come."

Paula looked at me and nodded. "I hope we can come that far."

"Oh, you'll be taking Karlie next year."

"Maybe we'll all go together," she said with hope. "It could be our tradition."

And we did. By New Years' Karlie was out of the hospital, back in high school and in regular therapy. A few years later, we were both bringing boyfriends and Karen drove on her own. Last year Paula retired but still offered me a ticket when opening night rolled around. Every year, no matter what else changed, Karlie, Paula, Karen and I watched Elizabeth dance across the stage and our hearts.

A Different Kind of Christmas

"Well, this is going to be quite the Christmas," Nancy said as Greg drove the LeSabre west across the Nebraska/Colorado state line. Nancy's sunglasses reflected the waves of brown grass and telephone wires on the bare Colorado prairie.

"You've been saying that the whole way," her husband responded. Fourteen hours to go from Skokie to eastern Colorado. Two days of Nancy's continual wondering what it would be like. You'd think she was five years old instead of a forty-eight-year-old woman. Greg would have given up what was left of his hair for one swig of strong whiskey.

"I am so glad we celebrated at home," she sighed. "To think that we're celebrating Christmas with Marti and the kids and all of us staying in her house. Not my idea of celebrating Christmas—spending it with your ex-wife and kids."

"The hotel closed," Greg said for the third time that day. "It doesn't make sense to drive twenty miles twice a day back to Sterling."

"No, I don't suppose it does," she agreed, "but it just seems like we're going to be on top of each other."

"No, not in that house. That house originally belonged to Marti's grandmother. They had nine kids and at least six bedrooms."

"Now why would a single woman want to live in a big old house like that?" Nancy said. "The heating bills must be out of sight."

"She had better memories there than in our house," Greg said with a shrug, remembering the fights in their ranch house. "Plus the kids loved visiting that house. We would find them over there any hour of the day."

Nancy sighed again. "I'm just so nervous about how this will go. I mean, Marti is nice enough, but for me, your wife, to stay with the ex-wife, just seems….rather uncomfortable."

Everything makes you nervous. You're nervous if you're driving with me. You're nervous when I am out on a trip with my rig. You're nervous when your granddaughter comes over to play because she might break something or hurt your damn dog. Now you're worried about hanging out with my ex-wife, my son and his family. But you'd worry even more if you stayed home.

"It's not about us," Greg said. "It's for Ryan and Heather and Rihanna. Heather said it would be good for Ryan to celebrate Christmas and bring back the old memories of the good times."

"Oh, I know. Your poor son has been through hell and back. I know."

You don't know. Greg lit another cigarette, holding the wheel steady with his knee. He never smoked so much as when he drove with Nancy. *I don't even know and I was in the service twenty years ago when we ran the bastard out of Kuwait. I didn't come home with one less arm, one less eye and no legs. We don't the hell know.*

"Did Heather say whether the nightmares stopped?" Nancy asked, breaking the silence.

"Why would they stop?" he asked. "It's not been that long."

"I just hoped they had." She stared out the window again.

Nancy and Greg had gone together to see Ryan in Walter Reed about six months ago but Nancy refused to go again. "It's too depressing," she said. "I'm not helping him any by being there, and I don't like kenneling Sasha." Greg had yelled but her decision relieved him of added stress. He went back five or six times when his boy was in rehab, and Greg could get a driving trip to DC from Skokie. His son didn't say much then but would sleep a lot until he would suddenly wake up, fighting battles.

When Greg had gotten the word about Ryan's injury, he'd been in a bar in Missoula, cooling his jets after a twelve hour drive and talking to the bar maid who seemed a little lonely. Nancy had called him after Marti had called her. *I will stop drinking if you let him live* was his promise/prayer to something/someone as he started back to Skokie that night. He thought afterwards he should have driven a tighter bargain about what kind of life Ryan would be getting in exchange for his father's giving up alcohol. When he got the guts to call Marti, she told him it was going to be touch and go all the way because of the blood loss. *I'll give up drinking if you let him live,* the six foot-four, muscular man prayed as he knelt down at the first rest stop in South Dakota. All the way home to Skokie and back to his wife, he repeated that mantra as he drove. He kept repeating it the next month as he waited for his son to come home.

Greg was still holding up his end of the bargain when Ryan arrived back in the States. He almost broke it after he saw his son the first time. Greg had driven twenty hours straight to see him and then it took all his strength to keep from running out the door when he saw Ryan lying there. Marti, a foot shorter than Greg, was able to hold him and kept him from running away.

Visiting him in the hospital marked the first time he had seen Marti since Ryan's wedding. She looked good, hair more red than he remembered, still feisty as ever, but she gave him a big hug when he came through the door of the room the first time. She was the one, like always, who held it together.

Gradually he got used to seeing his twenty-three-year-old son, lying there in a t-shirt with only one arm, the sheet covering his stumps that once were his legs. Sadly, there were guys in worse shape. Guys who didn't have families able to come or who chose not to. Marti took care of everyone in that ward; bringing them candy bars, helping them sit up if an aide wasn't readily available, just talking to them about things as if everything was normal. She held the ones whose girlfriends broke up via phone call or email. Greg brought them cigarettes until Heather asked "Are you finishing what the Taliban couldn't?"

His daughter-in-law was feisty like Marti. Rihanna, his four-year-old granddaughter, was a pistol. One day she was playing with the equipment still hooked up to Ryan and an alarm went off, causing staff to rush in. Ryan, who had been silent all morning, turned over and said "Who is that kid?" They all laughed, but Greg wondered if it was a joke or whether he truly didn't know.

Once Ryan was through the first months of therapy, Marti wanted them to come back to Wheaton to recuperate and start over, but Heather insisted that they would live in Colorado Springs so that they would be close to Fort Carson's services as well as where he had been stationed prior to deployment.

"What about Buckley?" Marti asked, referring to the military base in Denver, wanting them at least an hour closer.

"No, not good enough. Besides we have our apartment in Ft. Carson. It's where we can start back to being normal again." Petite, with long blond hair and blue eyes, Heather was a mighty warrior herself when it came to her husband of five years.

Normal? With one eye, one arm, and no legs? Greg didn't see normal happening too quickly. But he'd been out of Ryan's daily life since the kid was nine so there was no way of getting back into giving too straight forward suggestions, let alone commands.

While Greg eventually got used to the visible deformities, Ryan's brain injury and subsequent mental problems still threw him off. The nightmares were just the tip of the iceberg of pain looming over his son and his family. Ryan's speech, when he talked at all, often came in stops and stutters. He repeated himself, sometimes forgetting names or simple words. Rihanna was too small to really notice her father's lapses, but at times simple things shook Heather to her core.

"I went there three times today," Heather said one night in tears back at the hotel where Greg was staying. The cigarette shook in her hands. Greg didn't even know she smoked. "Tonight he said 'Where's my wife?' I said, 'I am right here, honey.'"

"'No, my wife! She's left me.'" The twenty-three-year-old caught her breath. "The saddest thing is," Heather said after crying for a few minutes, "is that I wonder where my husband is and if he'll ever come back."

Ryan and Heather met in kindergarten. Ryan came home smitten and later revealed to his parents that the missing toys, snacks, and treasured items had been offered up as tokens of affection. He towered over her in high school but his petite girlfriend ran the show. Marti described Heather as an orphan with living parents, making her a member of the family even before they were married. Marti kept Greg informed even when the kids weren't talking to him. Now Ryan's warrior wife took on the military complex who drug their feet on processing paperwork necessary for their move. She talked to politicians when they were in DC about the conditions the men were serving under and the care available when they were injured. She wrote thank you notes to everyone in Wheaton who took the time to send their well wishes.

When Marti said they would celebrate Christmas when Ryan was ready, Heather jumped on board. "Daddy will be home for Christmas," Heather told Rihanna. "Don't worry. Santa will find us wherever we're at, whenever your daddy's ready for Christmas." The little girl had nodded, big brown eyes wide with wonder at Santa's powers.

"I think it's a shame," Nancy said, interrupting his remembering. "The poor little girl will never remember her daddy normal and her mother…. while she's a saint when it comes to Ryan, Heather is expecting way too much of that little thing."

"I don't know," Greg said. "Heather is a sweetheart. If she stays with him, Ryan will do ok."

"Of course, she'll stay with him," Nancy insisted. "That's what you do when you get married, for better or for worse." She laid her head down on the shoulder of her husband of two years, evidently forgetting her two past husbands.

I hope she's seen the worse. Greg was the only one besides Heather who knew about the time that Ryan had almost choked his wife to death. Greg came in to find his son with the left arm pulled tight around his wife throat. The kid was like a mad man. It seemed to be forever before he could pull his daughter-in-law out of the grip, both flopping down on the floor. Then while they all caught their breath, some type of normalcy came back to Ryan who started crying.

"Don't say anything," Heather gasped.

"You need to tell the doctors," Greg said once his heart stopped racing. "That was dangerous— he could—." He didn't finish the thought but his mind raced to the four-year-old down the hall.

"I don't think he would," Heather said, knowing what they were both thinking. After that, she kept a bottle of pepper spray inside her waist band, hooked to her belt loop. She didn't let Rihanna be with him alone.

That horrible night was the last time he had seen his son, daughter-in-law and granddaughter. Marti had extended the invitation to celebrate Ryan's arrival back in Colorado and Christmas all at the same time. Once again, she had saved Greg from slipping away from his son, even if it meant sharing some of the sad old times. Marti was the one who held them together.

After an hour more of driving and three additional expressions of concern on whether Sasha would eat at the kennel, whether Rihanna would like her present, and whether that mole on Nancy's right hip was changing, the couple arrived at the house of his ex-wife. He smiled when he saw the lights on the evergreen bushes and the reindeer on top of the roof. Marti met them on the wrap around porch of the century old white house. Her smile was as warm as the afternoon.

"Hello," she said, hugging them both. "I am so glad you came."

Marti was the one who had ended their marriage and had told him to leave town. "It's the drinking," she said. "I love you but I can't see you destroying yourself in front of the kids."

For the next three years, he drank even more and still more when he was married to Elsa. She was doing drugs and other men so Greg didn't see the kids as much during those two years. He met Nancy after Elsa skipped town with Greg's paycheck and ten pounds of quality grass. Nancy was working at a truck stop outside of Ely, Nevada. She seemed to think there was enough substance to him that it was worth taking the chance or else she just wanted something different than serving coffee and eggs every day. He agreed and paid for their move to Skokie, bringing them closer to her daughter and granddaughter in Chicago. Nancy scolded him about the drinking but didn't threaten to leave so his drinking continued until he got the call about Ryan. *I should have asked for more.*

"Are they here?" he asked Marti.

"Not yet. We've got a surprise for Ryan so Heather's not leaving until five or so. It will be dark by the time they get here."

"Driving after dark is a good way to hit a deer," he said.

"You going to tell her that?" Marti smiled. "With what she's faced, a deer on the road is the least of her worries. Plus you're a good one to talk. You drove straight through from Chicago to get to DC when he arrived. How many deer did you hit?"

"I got more tickets than deer," he said looking up at the house. "You put the reindeer up on the roof yourself?"

His little ex-wife whacked him on the head. "No, Santa did. Who else is crazy enough to do that?"

He hugged her again. "You look good." Marti had lost twenty pounds through this ordeal, but was still carrying about thirty more than she should. Her hair now had gray showing around the edges, and her blue shirt was spotted with grease stains. She was not the homecoming queen he had dated in high school, but it was obvious that she didn't care, nor did he.

"Thanks. Nancy, you got your hair cut. I like it." Marti smiled genuinely at her successor. Greg recognized the unspoken criticism. *Don't rave about the old wife in front of the new one.*

"Thanks. I thought it was time to start looking my age." Nancy blushed at the compliment. She had hemmed and hawed about whether to cut her long hair or not, wondering if Marti would look better to Greg than she did.

"Let me show you where you're staying. I am giving the kids my room. Us old ones will have to climb the stairs." Marti led them inside the familiar building.

"Maybe I'll lose weight," Nancy said, breathing a little harder as they went up the impressive oak staircase. "Go with my new look."

"Oh—I didn't tell you—Sara came home last night," Marti said as she paused in front of a door.

"Does she know I am here?" Greg asked.

"Of course," Marti said.

"That's a surprise."

"Oh, Greg," Nancy said, "I am sure she's forgiven you."

Greg shook his head. His daughter had sworn never to speak to him again. *I don't blame her. I wouldn't forgive me either.*

"Is she home now?" he asked.

"No, she went to see Tracy. After six years of being gone, and Tracy married, they're still best friends."

It happened at Sara's high school graduation. When Marti divorced him, Sara, 14, had taken his part while his son was still a mama's boy at 11. There had been a couple of missed events, but Sara still believed him and believed in him. He had gotten back to town the night before commencement and met up with Rollie Nelson, his former best friend and now the town drunk. They had partied with some kids, and he smoked some weed. The party was starting again the next day when he remembered why he had come to Wheaton. At three p.m. he raced to the gym just when Sara was coming on stage to give her valedictorian speech.

"Baby," he yelled as he rushed the stage before she had started speaking. "I made it." Then he fell off the stage.

Sara didn't miss a beat with her speech as the principal and the basketball coach helped Greg up. That day marked when Ryan and Sara both stopped doing anything with him. He was with Elsa and even more wasted most weekends. Luckily, the cops never caught him driving stoned or drunk.

Ryan got back in touch with a wedding invitation but Sara stayed as far away from him as she could in the church and at the city hall for the reception. The last straw was when she left the family wedding picture when Marti invited him to be in it.

I don't know what else to give up, but please let my daughter forgive me. He started a new pack of cigarettes. Greg didn't think he could make it through this impromptu Christmas without his cigarettes. *One miracle at a time.*

"So I put you in Ryan's old room," Marti said, "but I've moved all the stuff downstairs—at least the stuff I thought he'd like to have around. Closet has clothes in it. I need to go through it sometime and get rid of things, but I just haven't."

"So what can we do to help?" Nancy asked.

"Would you make the cranberry relish and I'll get the eggnog mixed?"

"I'd be glad to," Nancy said. "You coming?"

"No," Greg said. "I am going to look around a little bit."

There were the scrapbooks that Marti's mother had started for the kids: pictures of them little, and then pictures of when Ryan was in Boy Scouts. Then there was a picture of Ryan graduating. By this time, Marti's mother was in the nursing home, but Marti kept the book up. There was his military picture, along with the wedding picture that had been in the paper.

There was a newspaper clipping from the Sterling paper about the attack. He had read it before, but this time he couldn't bring himself to read it again so he flipped back to the first part of the book. He found a picture of himself running after Ryan on a bike.

There were few pictures of the kids with Marti. Probably because she was the one always taking the pictures. Even if she wasn't in the pictures there were no questions about who had been most present in their lives.

"Greg," Nancy called. "Come down here please."

He walked into the kitchen where the women were sitting at the table.

"What?"

"We need three apples for the relish," Marti said. "I had three, but Sara must have eaten a couple. Would you go get them?"

He frowned a bit. "Pat still own the grocery store?"

"Yeah," Marti said, "but I don't think he'll bite you."

"He threatened to do worse to me when I left you."

"I left you," she said. "He knows that."

"Guess I'll see him sooner or later with Ryan being here."

"Yeah, they're all planning to come by tomorrow."

"Makes more sense than driving to Sterling," he said unconvincingly.

"Yes, it does," Nancy said.

"Does he still have that Rottweiler at the store?"

"No," Marti said. "Just his old shotgun." Then the two started laughing.

"Who is Pat?" Nancy asked.

"My brother—he was the best man at our wedding. Look, Greg," Marti said earnestly, "Pat isn't going to cause a scene because he adores Ryan and he knows Ryan wants you here."

"Ok, but if I am not back in half an hour, someone come looking for me."

"'Oh, we will," Nancy giggled.

For someone nervous about coming, she's gotten incredibly comfortable. The store was only three blocks from the house so he walked it. More stores were empty, but at least there were two or three cars in front of the IGA. He came in slowly, wondering if Pat would be behind the meat counter. His brother-in-law could use a knife pretty well.

"Can I help you," a young woman said, from behind the cash register.

"Jamie?"

Her eyes narrowed. "Uncle Greg! You came!"

The 18-year-old hugged him. "I am surprised that you recognize me. It's been a long time."

"Oh, I'd know you anywhere. You used to give me the best piggy back rides. I saw Sara a couple of hours ago."

"Your dad here?" Greg ignored the comment about his daughter.

"Yeah, he's in the back."

"I'll see you tomorrow, ok?" He gave her a quick smile.

"You betcha." She hugged him before he could leave.

He walked back to the door behind the meat counter. "What's it take to get some service?" he called out, then wondered if his brother-in-law would appreciate his sense of humor.

"What the hell?" Pat Taylor came to the front. "Oh, you sonofabitch!" Then he stuck his hand out. "It's good to see you, man."

"Yeah, you too."

The two embraced uncomfortably as men sometimes do. "So is Ryan home?" Pat asked.

"No, I guess they're coming in late. Some kind of surprise."

"Yeah, I know about the surprise."

"Will he like it?"

"I think so. He used to like it a lot," the older man took a step back, looking at his ex-brother-in-law. "You look good, man. You look like you put on some weight and aren't the skinny runt you used to be." Pat was carrying probably more than 20 pounds since Greg had seen him last, but the face was the same.

"I stopped drinking," Greg said. "I had my last drink when I got the word about Ryan."

"That's what—nine months ago? Like having a baby."

"Yeah, it was early September."

"It's a horrible way to stop drinking, but you look good. I am glad you came back for this." Out of character, he gave Greg a genuine hug.

"You look good too," Greg said, pulling a bit away but smiling. His brother-in-law had Marti's strong blue eyes, but had a belly going over his belt.

Pat shrugged. "I don't know. I'd sell the store if I could find a buyer, but out here, that's not going to happen. I guess I'll keep working until Jamie graduates from college. Saw Sara a little while ago….she's looking good too."

"Yeah," he lied. "Just like her mother."

Pat snorted. "Right—especially the hair."

"I better get what I came down for or Marti will wonder if you killed me."

"I haven't threatened to do that for ten years at least. Just take what you need."

Funny how Ryan's injury seemed to have smoothed over the hurt with his brother-in-law. "Ok, see you tomorrow."

He got the apples and started feeling lighter knowing than Pat was happy to see him. They had played football together and had a lot of good times before the troubles between him and Marti began. His brother-in-law had thrown a punch or two after the last big fight he and Marti had, but evidently it was now in the past. Greg was on the last block of Main Street when someone called his name.

"Greg Tucker, is that you?" A pudgy man waddled from the Blue Moon Bar across the street to catch up with him.

"Hey, Larry. How are you?" Greg said with a small wave. "Still the mayor?"

"Yeah, still the mayor." Sweat pooled at his armpits. "Didn't know whether you'd be back for this or not."

"Of course, I am back," Greg said in a curt voice. "I am here for Ryan and Heather and Rihanna."

"Well, I just got news that Channel 7 from Denver is going to cover it," the mayor said gleefully. "We're waiting for Channel 9 to get back to us."

"Cover what?" Greg asked with a sinking feeling.

"Cover Ryan's homecoming—and the fact that we're celebrating Christmas in June. Damn it, didn't you know that?"

"I knew we were, but I didn't know the town was."

"God, man. Didn't you notice the lights?" Larry pointed overhead. "We're going to have Christmas tomorrow! Reverend Hoster is going to have a Christmas program at the church tomorrow night."

"Whose idea was that?"

"Mine," Larry beamed. "I am doing as much as I can to welcome back the wounded hero home. Of course, it helps put Wheaton on the map too."

"Does Marti know about it?"

"Well….she knows we were putting the lights up," he scratched at the back of his neck. "And she didn't seem to care if Hoster did the service. I didn't tell her about the news being here."

"Maybe you should have," Greg said, moving away from the sweaty man.

"Well, hey, let me buy you a drink," Larry said, cocking his head back to the Blue Moon. "Father of the war hero and everything!"

"No, thanks." He swallowed a mouth full of dust. "I quit drinking."

Larry stared and let out a guffaw. "You? Ten Gallon Greg?"

"Yep. Nine months now," Greg said, flinching at the old nickname. "Look, I gotta go take these apples back to the house. Nice talking to you, Larry."

He walked fast back to the house with the needed apples. Nancy and Marti were still in the kitchen, talking over coffee, as if they were long lost friends.

"Hey, hon," Nancy said, "did you know that Marti and I were born in the same month?"

"Yeah, I knew that…" He turned to Marti. "What's the deal with the whole town celebrating Christmas?"

"I didn't tell them to do that," Marti said a bit defensively. "I just told Pat, who's on the chamber of commerce. He got the city to string up the lights. Then a few guys told me that they'd decorate their houses too as part of it. What's the big deal?"

"Larry Williams just told me that the TV news is covering Ryan's homecoming."

"They are?" Her voice rose in emotion for the first time since they arrived.

"Wonderful!" Nancy said smiling. "I think that's great."

Greg and Marti glared at her happy face. "You got to be kidding. Ryan's not ready for that! This was going to be a quiet, family celebration," Marti said frustrated, rubbing her brow. "Not some circus."

"Oh, it will be wonderful," Nancy said. "Everything will be great. I am sure he'll be excited about all the work people have done."

"I don't think so. I don't think it's what Heather had in mind." Marti looked even madder and sadder at the same time. "This isn't a good idea at all."

"Larry's an idiot. Don't you think he knew we would want Ryan to feel at home before we surprised him with Christmas?" He felt as helpless as he had in Walter Reed.

"Damn that Larry." Marti got up from the table and walked away.

He had never heard her curse anyone besides himself. She didn't even curse the bastard who bombed Ryan's convoy. He followed her out to the front porch where for a minute or two they stood in silence.

"Sara called," Marti told him before Greg came up with anything useful to say. "She has a flat tire but doesn't have a jack. Will you go over and change it? She's still at Tracy's."

He'd been hoping for a few distractions when his daughter finally got him in her sights. A flat tire and a news crew wasn't what he was hoping for, and he'd almost rather head back to Skokie than face his daughter. Part of A.A, however, was making amends so he just nodded and headed out the door.

Tracy lived about two miles out of town. Driving there felt as intimidating as when he drove into DC the night he saw Ryan for the first time. Their house was decorated up for Christmas even though Tracy's husband was still overseas with the rest of Ryan's unit. "Hey, Greg!" a very pregnant Tracy called out and met him before he got out of the car.

"Hey," he said with a weak smile. Sara and Tracy were closer than sisters so she didn't return the smile. He didn't doubt they each had the same opinion of him, but Tracy was always a little calmer. "Marti said Sara has a flat."

Tracy nodded. "She's inside, working on a welcome home poster for Ryan. You can come in, if you want."

Greg still wanted to turn tail and run but he followed Tracy inside anyway. A girl, no, a young woman with short spiked hair, streaked red, white and blue, sat at the dining room table drawing a on a large poster board. "Your dad's here," Tracy said, by way of introduction.

"Hey," was all he could get out.

Sara narrowed her eyes and stood up. Greg raised his hands, half in surrender, half hoping his little girl would magically forget everything he put her through. Sara stepped up to him and sniffed his breath. "Mom said you stopped drinking." It was the first sentence she'd spoken to him in years. "Is it true?"

31

"Yeah," Greg said. "Nine months."

She nodded, recognizing the pattern of events. She was wearing a brown t-shirt with the words Choose Peace. She had Marti's eyes, but his height and build. "Good," she said without any change in expression.

'The poster looks good," he offered sincerely. It was covered in stars and stripes with pictures of Ryan, Heather and Rihanna.

"I thought it'd be nice," she said, glancing down at it,

He nodded. "Guess I'd better go look at that tire."

"Guess so," Sara said, following him out the door.

She watched as he got the jack out of his trunk and began to remove the tire. Her mouth was pressed into a thin, irritated line of distaste and he squirmed under her glare. "It's good to see you," he said.

Sara shrugged. "I'm only doing this for Ryan. He wants you here. You do anything to make him not want you here, and I will gladly kick you out of town myself. No drinking, no drugs, no fighting with Mom. Ryan has enough to deal with."

"Ok," he said. He knew Sara had every reason to distrust him. If he ruined Ryan's homecoming, he'd deserve every punishment she gave him.

"Let's just get through this crazy Christmas thing," Sara said, crossing her arms as he removed the tire.

"Ok," he said again, wondering if the temporary cease fire would apply to next Christmas or just Ryan's homecoming. "It's a nice thing to do for Ryan. I hope the news crews don't bother him too much."

"What news crews?" Sara stared at him. He then told her about Larry's grandiose plan.

"Hell, that's all Ryan needs." Sara pushed her fingers through her patriotic hair, forgetting to be angry with her father. "He wouldn't have liked that before the accident. He sure as hell won't like it now. Now he might even have a panic attack."

"Yeah," he agreed. "Didn't seem right to me."

"It's not right!" Sara said savagely. "Like we haven't got enough to worry about without that hippo using Ryan as a tourist attraction!" She was still fuming as Greg secured the tire into place.

"Let's go!" She stalked around the car. "I gotta talk to Mom about this." She slammed the door behind her and pulled out without another word to her father.

His daughter drove like a madman, like he used to drive before his alcoholic's intuition told him one wrong swerve could land him in a prison cell. He ought to have thanked whoever he'd been praying to that she talked to him at all, but he felt like he'd swallowed a rock. Sara still hated him. Knowing his daughter hated him had been… maybe not comfortable in Skokie but at least it wasn't the first thought in his mind. Here, driving past the streets where they used to walk hand in hand, eating ice cream and talking about how she liked third grade, Sara's hatred cut him deep. He couldn't blame her.

He kept her in his sights until they got back into town then he took a left onto Main Street while she headed toward Marti's house. He parked in front of the Blue Moon Bar, next to the Channel 7 news van.

He staggered out of the LeSabre. He had to push on the bar's door twice to get in. "Jim, give me a drink," he yelled as he entered.

"What's up, Greg?" the bartender asked him, looking at him closely.

"Just give me a drink." His words slurred. The bartender poured him a draft.

Greg hadn't touched a beer in nine months. He never set foot in a bar, avoided the liquor section of the grocery store, and changed the channel when a beer commercial came on. Now he had a glass in his hand. The amber liquid never looked so beautiful in the dim light of the bar. His fingers quaked against the cold condensation.

"Ten Gallon Greg!" Larry Williams slapped him hard on the back. "I knew you'd be back! Stan, this is the father of our hometown hero, Greg Tucker. Greg, this is Stan Steadbedder of Channel 7 News!"

"Good to meet you," Stan Steadbedder said, offering his hand. "We're real honored to cover your son's homecoming."

"There won't be any homecoming," Greg said. "Ryan's not up to it."

"You unbelievable pig!" Sara shouted, pushing through the bar doors. "I can't believe I thought you'd changed!"

Greg swallowed. He could almost taste the beer through his fingers. "It doesn't matter," he said. "Ryan's not coming."

Sara came toward her dad but Larry stepped in front of her. "I'm sorry, Greg. I must have misheard. You didn't say that Ryan wasn't coming. Did you?" The mayor's face was a bright red.

Greg nodded and Sara dropped her purse with a thump. "Heather called. Said he can't make the trip. Maybe next week."

"Next week?" Larry sputtered.

"Or not," Greg added. "He's having a ...bad time of it lately."

"Next week is the Fourth of July!" Larry snapped. "We can't just... ignore the Fourth of July for some cr-"

"Watch it!" Sara snapped and Larry cut himself off with a frightened look.

"Sorry, Mr. Tucker," Stan Steadbedder said. "Mr. Williams, we can't wait around that long. Give us a call when he does come in. Maybe there's a human interest piece we can work out." He tossed a twenty on the bar and headed out with the rest of his crew.

"Damn!" Larry said, waddling after them with a spiel about the rest of Wheaton's newsworthy attractions.

Greg let out a breath he didn't know he'd been holding as the door slammed shut. Sara stared at him, her mouth open. "You want a beer?" he asked, pushing the glass toward her.

She sat down next to him and chugged it. "You just lied to the mayor," she said, wiping her mouth clean.

Greg nodded, instantly relieved that the temptation was gone. "I thought I could calm things down a little for Ryan."

"Smart," Sara said with an approving look.

"We ought to get back to your mother's," he said, placing the money on the bar. Sara nodded and followed him out the door.

Marti hugged them both when Sara told her what had happened. Then the next few hours were spent in hustle and bustle of the holiday, finishing up the food and calling friends and relatives. If it weren't for the heat, Greg would have thought it was really Christmas. Heather called when they reached Sterling at 10 p.m. By the time the SUV pulled into Wheaton, everyone else had been called. Marti's brother switched the street Christmas lights on and people stood on Main Street, waving flags as the SUV drove by.

The family unloaded quietly at Marti's. "Did he say anything about the lights?" Nancy asked Heather.

She shook her head. "He just looked at them."

They all followed Marti into the living room where Ryan sat in a straight back chair. His hair was as short as Sara's, but there were scars where no hair grew. His left eye was bright blue, like his mother and daughter's, and the patch he wore showed signs of Rihanna's art work. He stared ahead while Heather fiddled with Rihanna's long hair.

The crèche and the large candles were out just like Marti always had done, but the tree was different than what Greg remembered. It was a Charlie Brown type of tree. Sara had cut white doves which hung with new red and blue ornaments. Marti had put it on a table, but it stood only three feet high. One side was almost bare from when Murray, the dog, had chewed it up years ago. It was the Christmas Eve they spent at the vet.

"Rihanna," Nancy said, "I brought you something that Santa left at my house for you."

"I thought we'd open presents in the morning, like we always did for Christmas," Marti said.

"It's not really Christmas," Rihanna said. "This is different."

They looked to her mother for guidance. "Ok," Heather said. "Then it's time for bed."

Nancy went to the Christmas tree and pulled out a box wrapped in silver paper with silver bows. "Santa doesn't wrap presents," Ryan mumbled, his first words since coming in.

The little girl sprinted over to Nancy, grabbed the present and tore off the wrapping paper to reveal a Barbie wearing a blue flowing dress. Rihanna frowned but said nothing.

"Don't you like it?" Nancy said when the little girl just kept staring at it.

"I guess but I already have some Barbies. This is just another one. I wanted something different."

"What do you say?" Heather prompted. "What do you tell Nancy?"

"She didn't bring it; Santa did." Rihanna looked confused. Her hair was mussed, probably from sleeping in the car. Greg guessed it was far past her bedtime. "He brought me a Barbie last year too. At my house."

"But Grandma Nancy brought it here, helping Santa out. That counts for something," Marti said.

The little girl spoke in a small dutiful voice. "Thank you, Grandma Nancy."

"You're very welcome!" Nancy beamed. Rihanna yawned.

"Hey, kiddo," Sara said, crouching down to eye level with the little girl. "Want to sleep with me in my room? I hid some cookies up there."

"Yeah," Rihanna giggled and then looked seriously at her mom. "Can I?"

"Just tonight," Heather said. "But don't talk all night because we have to open presents in the morning."

"Ok…." they both said together and ran upstairs.

"Which one is the kid?" Marti said.

"I am not sure," Greg said, "but it is great to see them together."

"Funny…." Ryan whispered sounding confused.

"What's funny, honey?" Heather said. Then she laughed and stroked his head.

"Everything," he said. "Christmas in summer?

"Just this time," Marti said. "I wanted to have Christmas with you and Rihanna and Heather and we couldn't do it in December."

He nodded. "I was in the hospital."

"That's right, baby," Heather said.

"Not a baby," Ryan said. "A soldier."

"The best," she said.

"Not anymore," Ryan said, looking down to where his legs used to be. Sleek prosthetics allowed him some mobility but nowhere near the movement he had before. "Not anything anymore."

Heather pressed a kiss to his cheek. "You're a daddy and my husband, and still the best."

He shook his head. "Not anymore." The room was absolutely still.

"Ahhh….. I am getting tired," Nancy said, breaking the silence "Think I'll turn in before Santa comes."

"I am tired too," Heather said. "Come on, baby, let's go to bed."

"Not yet," Ryan said.

"I'll stay up and we'll talk," Greg said.

"Are you sure?" Heather looked a little nervous and tired.

"It will be …." Ryan thought for a minute, "ok….different."

"Alright," Heather leaned over and kissed him. "Don't be long; I can't sleep without you."

Nancy came over and kissed Greg. "Night, honey. Come to bed soon, ok? She turned to go up the stairs and then went back to Ryan. "Good to have you home." She kissed him, surprising the soldier.

"Who is that?" he said when she left the room.

"That's Nancy, my wife," Greg said with a smile.

"I thought Mom was your wife." His son looked confused.

"When you were born, I was his wife," Marti said, "but then we divorced."

"And then I married Nancy," Greg said.

"But don't forget Elsa," Sara said, coming back into the room.

"Oh…. pothead." Ryan grinned.

"Yeah," Sara sat on the arm of his chair. "Remember the last time we went to Dad's and found her dope."

"Yeah. Good stuff. What happened to it?"

"I threw it away," Marti said. "You guys were too young to have that. What were you thinking?" she said, looking at Greg.

"Got me. I guess I wanted some excitement."

"Proud of you," Ryan said. "I am proud of you."

Greg felt his heart in his throat. *Not as much as I am of you.*

Sara came over to where Ryan was sitting and leaned over and pulled him up. "Hug me," she said.

The one-armed soldier followed orders and without any other words, Marti joined in quickly but Greg stood on the sidelines, not sure if he'd be welcomed. Then Ryan said, "Dad…" and Sara gave him a quick nod and he joined the circle.

"It feels good," Marti said after a couple of minutes, "but we all need to get to bed. Or Rihanna will be jumping on the beds at four a.m. waking us up."

Ryan nodded. "It's good." He hobbled off to the downstairs bathroom. Sara sucked in her breath watching him go, and a little tremble passed through her shoulder, and then an earthquake. Greg put his arm around her and she buried her face in his shoulder. "He'll be alright," he whispered.

"I don't know…." she shook as she whispered.

"He'll be alright."

They stood for a quiet moment, father and daughter for the first time in years. Sara pulled away first, wiping her eyes. "I gotta go to bed," she said.

"Goodnight," he said. She didn't reply, but touched his shoulder, and then went up the stairs. He looked out the picture window in the living room. Across the street, three houses with Christmas lights twinkled. It was good to be in Marti's house.

In the middle of the night Greg heard the wind come up. Then there was a loud bang, followed by a flash of light. Summer thunderstorm in Colorado. Then there was a scream from the downstairs bedroom, followed by a howl. Greg raced down the stairs, followed by Marti.

Sara held Rihanna. "Wait baby," she said at the top of the landing. Nancy wandered slowly behind them

"Hey, it's alright," Greg said, coming out of the room. "The storm just woke him up rough."

In a short time, a shaken Heather came out with Ryan on his stump braces.

"Sorry," she said. "I think we're ok."

"Just the thunder and the wind. Listen; it's raining now," Marti said.

"I don't know how Santa got here without any snow for the sleigh," Rihanna said barely able to speak, but eyes were peeking around her aunt.

"Magic," Sara said. "Santa can do anything." She knelt down and scooped her niece up and went back to bed.

"You ok, Heather?" Marti asked.

"I think so," she said a little shaky. "I just never know what to expect or when to expect it."

"I'll be here," Greg said, grabbing a pillow off the couch and laying down on the hallway's floor.

Marti reached into a cabinet and pulled out a light sheet. "It might be a little cooler in the morning."

The house quieted down again, but Greg didn't fall asleep. Or he didn't think he had, but then there were two voices out on the landing. "Now?" Rihanna asked in a loud whisper.

"Yes, it's six o'clock," Sara said. "You can wake them up."

"Wake up! Wake up!" Rihanna's voice rang throughout the hallway above him, and Sara pounded on doors. "Time to get up!"

Greg hadn't even gotten off the floor when the four-year-old jumped on him. "Did you see Santa?" Rihanna squealed.

"No, he only comes when we're all asleep." Greg had told his children the same thing years ago.

"Where are the presents?" the little girl demanded gleefully

"Right in here," Sara said. "I'll bring you coffee, Dad. You too, Jerk." Ryan stood with Heather in the doorway, looking drowsy.

Greg looked past where his son and daughter-in-law came from. The bedroom was torn apart. "We need to start the morning a little calmer," Heather said, "but it's ok now."

"Let's see what Santa brought," Marti said and they went into the formal living room.

"Chocolate covered cherries," Greg said opening his present from Sara. "Where did you find them this time of year?"

"Freezers. They keep for a long time."

"I want one," Ryan said. "Remember when…..."

'Yeah, we had two boxes; one for me, and one for you….and the dog ate mine. What was that dog's name?" Greg asked. Another Christmas Eve at the vet's.

"Moonray," Ryan said.

"No, it was Murray, but you called it Moonray," Sara said.

"Moonray. Better name," Ryan said. "I called you Freak."

"Yeah, Jerk."

The presents were a wide assortment—place mats for Marti from Greg and Nancy; Avon products for Sara and Heather, t-shirts for Ryan. More toys for Rihanna from a bike to an extensive set of doll clothes.

Rihanna did not seem too taken in with this. "I don't want a bike," she said to Marti. "I am too little."

"You're just right," Marti said. "This summer we'll go riding in the park near your house. Daddy's going to ride his bike as well, according to his doctor."

Ryan was equally blasé about the whole doings. "Got an artificial tree," he said looking at it. "How come?"

"It's hard to get a tree in June, and I thought it would get too dry," Marti sounded as if she was tearing up with the failure of her event.

"Wasn't that your mom's tree?" Greg said. She nodded.

"Different," Ryan said.

"Special," Heather said. "It's different, but special."

"I got you something, Daddy," Rihanna stood up and raced upstairs. She was back in a flash with a white washcloth, covering something held in her hands. "Here, Daddy."

He unwrapped the cloth and held it in his left hand.

"Daddy," Rihanna said proudly, "I made it last night."

Nancy saw it first and gasped. "Why you little…." and burst into tears.

There was the doll that Nancy had brought Rihanna, minus an arm and both legs cut midway. The hair was cut off spiky, like Sara's, and one eye was marked out with black felt marker. She wore a green sock over her torso with part of a black shoe string tied around its waist. Greg felt Nancy, Heather and Marti all tremble as if the four-year-old had punched them in the gut.

"She's a warrior," Rihanna said proudly, not noticing the adult reaction. "Just like my daddy."

Sara reached out and tousled Rihanna's hair. "That's right, baby,"

Ryan smiled, and laid it in his lap. "Special ….." he said, reaching to touch his daughter's cheek, "and different."

The Saint of Mount Vista Retirement Community

By early September Danielle wondered why she had ever moved to Greeley. Oh, there was tons more to do in Greeley—concerts, music, lectures at the University. But Danielle didn't have time, money or anyone to go with to the social events. Greeley still smelled like cows, just like the big feedlots near the small town of Pershing, South Dakota. She had hoped Greeley would be the John Denver type of Colorado that her dad used to sing about. She had hoped her uncle would be like her father.

In fairness to Greeley, it was made up of the same working type of people who lived around her hometown, just more of them. There were cowboys, just like at home. Unlike her home town, there was a large meat packing plant—ColBeef. ColBeef had been the place where her uncle had worked, and where he said, if it weren't for the "goddamn Africans and Mexicans", she would have been able to get a job.

"They'll work for nothing," he said. "They'll live in a two bedroom apartment with eighteen or nineteen people. The union can't do anything about it. They're being paid squat. It's not like it was during the day."

The day was back when Carl had worked at ColBeef. He had worked there until 2002 when luck or non-luck, depending upon your perspective, had a side of beef knock him over, and screw up his back. "The union took care of me," Carl said. "They got me eighty per cent of my whole salary. With SSDI, I'm good."

That was when Aunt Dorothy went back to work. She worked at a nursing home, Mount Vista Retirement Community, which is where Danielle ended up. As the newest hire, Danielle had the night shift.

Danielle didn't mind the night shift. It gave her the excuse to sleep during the day when Carl was awake. Then it was only during the weekends that she had to avoid Carl.

He wasn't bad to her. It wasn't that. In fact, Carl told her that if she ever needed a ride home, to let him know and he'd come get her. He looked like her father, only more heavyset with a red face. Carl's nose was the nose of a drinker and his belly shook when he laughed. Her dad hadn't had a nose or a waist like his brother's, but he certainly liked drinking. Carl liked drinking, but not as much as her father. Carl didn't seem to like other people as much as her dad did, just the guys that he had worked with at the plant.

Her father liked everyone, so much that he'd buy the whole bar a drink—unlike her uncle who looked at her funny if she had two Mountain Dews in a day. It was after one of those nights of meeting people and buying drinks that Mike Pearson dropped dead on the way home. The autopsy indicated it was a heart attack. With his death, the idea of going to college went away just like all of Mike's friends. The cost of his funeral ate up the money she had saved for college. Danielle's mother told her she could come live with her, but that lasted only a week.

"Come out to Colorado," Aunt Dorothy had said at the funeral. "You can live in Cassie's room now that she's gone." Cassie was their daughter who had left Colorado to go to college and only came back at Christmas. Although three years older than Danielle, the cousins had been close growing up. Now the cousins hadn't seen much of each other and it felt funny to be in a room that she once had loved, with Cassie's pictures and trophies, but it was still better than being with her mother.

"Yeah, it's hell of a lot better than South Dakota," Carl had said. "Never stays cold long and, shoot, you could take some classes at UNC."

So she had left Pershing in August, with the idea that she would work in Greeley and then go to school when she had money saved up. She had tried to get a job at the college, but the only work they had went to students. She was glad that ColBeef wasn't hiring so that she didn't have to deal with the blood and the corpses. By the fourth week, when she hadn't found a job on her own, her uncle got terribly annoying.

"You can't just wait for something to come your way," he said. "That was what your dad did and look what happened to him."

That day Danielle went to work with her aunt. "Theresa, this is my niece that I was telling you about," Dorothy told the manager of the home.

"Have you ever worked with older people?" the woman asked, without smiling.

"No, I haven't," Danielle said, embarrassed.

"Well, the night shift starts at midnight. You can't go drinking before it starts, and come here and try to work." The woman said it very sternly, sounding like the judge in Dad's last DUI case before he died. "No partying. It puts the patients at risk."

"I don't party," Danielle said. "I don't know anyone here."

45

"Alright, I'll give you a shot, but just because you are Dorothy's niece." Theresa nodded and Danielle followed her to the office for paperwork.

That was how she started. The majority of the residents lived on the nursing care side. At midnight most of the residents were or should have been sleeping. The cleaning crew vacuumed up and down the hallways, washing spots of spilled food and bodily fluids off the walls, and did the laundry. Most of the women were Latina, as old as Aunt Dorothy, with worn hands and tired eyes. The woman in charge, Anahi, spoke to them in Spanish but to Danielle in English. She at least smiled.

"I want you to work with Maria. She's new too," Anahi told Danielle after all the papers had been signed.

The young woman with dark eyes smiled at her. "Habla Ingles?" Danielle asked, pulling out the little Spanish she had learned in high school.

"Un poco. ¿Habla Español?" Maria asked.

Danielle shook her head.

"Then you'll get lots done," Anahi said, smiling. "I want the dining room scrubbed spotless. Table 4 looks as if they've been having food fights again." She then repeated in Spanish to Maria.

They worked together quietly. It felt clean already to Danielle, but her father hadn't been one to keep things clean so maybe she didn't really know what clean was. She hadn't felt the need either. After her parents divorced, the table got cleared only when her mother came home every few weeks.

"It's a pig sty," her mother said. "You live as if you're in a barn." Even after her mother had left her and her dad, the house still mattered to her.

Her aunt's house was fairly clean. Her uncle smoked only in the living room and out on the patio. Danielle liked the smell of the cigarettes; it reminded her of her father.

Anahi looked over their work the first hour. "Bien," she said smiling. "Good. You two will do. I want you to do Doctor Kabisky's room too. It's a special case."

"I wouldn't think they would want their rooms done at night," Danielle said confused. "Aren't they sleeping at midnight?"

"Hopefully yes, but we make an exception for Hanna Kabisky. She plays the piano at one a.m. and that's when you'll clean the room.

Hanna Kabisky had the biggest room on the assisted living wing at the very end of the hall where the residents were most able to function independently. They could come and go as they pleased, but the staff cleaned and assisted whenever they were called. Most of the residents seldom called, liking to pretend that they were in apartments instead of an old folks' home.

The rest of the rooms on that wing were dark, but the one that looked like it was the biggest room had a light on behind the door. Anahi knocked and said softly, "Hanna, there's some people I want you to meet."

"Dr. Kabisky," the little woman in a blue suit said to the three as they stood outside. She spoke with a slight accent that Danielle couldn't place, except that it was different from Anahi and the other ladies' accented English.

"Yes, I am sorry, Dr. Kabisky. This is Danielle and Maria. They'll be cleaning your room during the week as we discussed, while you're practicing."

The little woman smiled and then Anahi smiled as well. "Lovely," the woman said. Without another word, she left the room and walked down the hall.

"What kind of doctor is she?" Danielle asked curious

"Eye doctor," Anahi said. "Very gifted. She used to have her piano in her room. But the other residents complained about her piano playing so late at night so she practices at one a.m. in the lounge before she goes to sleep."

"Why don't they clean the room at the normal time?" Danielle asked.

"The doctor does not want interruptions. She doesn't really mingle much and cleaning was a disruption. No talking. Get to work."

The suite was almost spotless, but Anahi showed them how to do it as if it was in desperate need of cleaning. The three took almost forty-five minutes without talking or stopping.

"There," the supervisor said finally. "Danielle, go down and get Dr. Kabisky and we'll make sure that we did it good enough for her. She's in the far lounge."

Danielle had vacuumed in there earlier. There were a few bookcases and an aquarium, but the main focus was an elegant grand piano. There sat Dr. Kabisky playing quietly. For a moment Danielle forgot what she was to do.

"That's beautiful," she said when the woman finally stopped.

"Thank you." She said it simply, bowing her head.

"You could have been a concert pianist."

"I was an ophthalmologist," she said proudly. "I was the only ophthalmologist who did surgery in Greeley for years."

"Eyes," Danielle said.

"Yes, the thing that you miss the most when you don't have them. I performed 5,023 operations in my time here," Dr. Kabisky said.

"That's a lot."

"It is a lot," she said, "and I'd still be doing it except my eyes aren't as good, but when you get to eighty-nine, what do you expect?"

Your room is done," Danielle said, not sure how to answer that. "Would you please come down and check it?"

"Why yes, I would."

She walked down and this time held the railing. At one point she stopped to catch her breath and then walked again.

"It smells clean," she said to Anahi when entering. The doctor touched a few things and looked carefully at an old picture of a young woman with a baby and smiled.

"Will this do?" Anahi asked after a minute.

"I believe it will. Thank you for accommodating me," the little lady said to Anahi. "These girls will do."

"Let me know if they don't do well," Anahi said. "They'll start cleaning at one a.m. as we agreed."

"Yes," Dr. Kabisky said, then her eyes suddenly brightened. "Oh, Anahi, do you know your name is from Persia?"

"No, Doctor, I didn't. I thought I was named after my grandmother who died in Mexico."

"Well, according to my research, it comes from a name called Anahita which means immaculate one. So you've really found a calling. Have a good evening, ladies."

At one in the morning every day, Dr. Kabisky would walk down to the area that had the beautiful piano in it. Sometimes she would start out with something bright and majestic and eventually go to something almost like a prayer. She played for the entire time they cleaned her room. Other staff sometimes would take a cup of coffee and listen to her. No one clapped; that would be like clapping in a church service, but they would nod as they took their brooms and mops out of the area to the sound of Debussy. When the two young women finished, Danielle would go down and inform her.

"How did you learn to play so wonderfully?" Danielle asked her one day as they walked back to the room after a particularly moving piece.

"Ah, I play nothing like my mother. She was a concert pianist in Prague. My father was a doctor so I became one. I wasn't good enough to become a pianist like her, but I enjoyed the lessons she gave me. She told me my skills were elsewhere. So I became a doctor like my father. I still play piano though. It helps me keep my fingers and brain going."

She did not look like any of the other residents. Her hair was always coifed in an elaborate French roll. She wore dresses or suits with a fine string of pearls, instead of smocks or slacks.

"She thinks she's something, that one," Pam, the only other native English-speaking aide on the graveyard shift, said. "Just because she brought that piano in and got the bigger room."

Pam had been born and raised in Greeley. She had dropped out of high school when she became pregnant. When the marriage didn't work, she was back living with her parents. After one attempt to clean Dr. Kabisky's room, she had been told not to return.

"She's a doctor," Danielle said. "She did eye surgery."

"Maybe but that was long ago. Now she's just like everyone except she doesn't have to play by all the rules. She's just a little old rich Jew who runs this place like they were really someone who matters. If Theresa knew what Anahi was doing, she'd stop it."

"Why don't you like her music?" Danielle asked.

"It's snotty. I want something I can sing to," she said before leaving to take a smoke.

When Danielle got home that morning, Dorothy was making coffee. "How was work, sweetie?" she said as the girl came in. "Can I make you breakfast?"

"Yeah, that would be great. Aren't you going to work today?"

"No. Carl has a doctor's appointment and I am going with him. He's talking with Frankie now, an old union buddy."

"Dorothy, do you know Dr. Kabisky?"

"Of course," she said. "Everyone knows her."

"I mean, did you know her when she was a doctor?"

"As a matter of fact I did. She was Carl's doctor."

"Really? When was that?"

"Back around 1998. He was mowing in the backyard, and got hit in the face with a piece of wire, cut his eye badly. Union warned him not to tell the company how he did it because he called in sick that day to mow the lawn. There were bad feelings at that time, and they would have used any excuse to get rid of a union man. She operated on his eye and saved it. He went back to work after three days. If he had lost it, we would have lost everything because it happened at home when he should have been working. We would have lost the house and all the savings for college. He'd have been fired for lying about being sick. She was a saint because she let us pay out of pocket for a few years instead of demanding the money at once."

"Who is a saint?" Carl said as he came in with his buddy.

"Dr. K," she said.

He shrugged. "What are you shrugging for?" Dorothy asked. "She saved your eye."

"Yeah...maybe. Maybe not."

"Carl, have you forgotten how bad it was?" she said. "She took you and we paid $100 a month to pay for the surgery."

"Yeah, well, she was a rich Jew," Frankie said, echoing Pam from earlier. "She could afford to do that."

"And on me, she got richer." Karl and Frankie laughed while Danielle felt her skin crawl.

"You know, I heard she donated a bunch of money to the Sudan house; you know that crapola group that's funding a place for those guys from Africa." Frankie lit a cigarette and sat down where Dorothy had been sitting.

"Why the hell would a Jew want to build a house for them in Greeley?" Carl asked in a curious voice. "Those Muslims would want to kill her more than anyone else."

"Maybe it's not just her eyes going batty," Frankie said, tapping his head.

Dorothy shook her head. "She's a saint. You're both batty. Get your own breakfast." She walked out of the room without making another comment.

Carl looked at his niece. "Why do you ask about her?" he said.

"I just see her every night. She's always good to me."

"Yeah, I thought so too. But I heard from some guys that she's been giving lots of money to the ACLU. They're a bunch of nuts, you know. Trying to change everything that maybe shouldn't be changed." He took a cigarette from his pack. "Always trying to change things isn't the way to go."

Danielle finished her breakfast in her room.

The next night when she came down to let Dr. Kabisky know that the room was done, she took a breath. "Doctor," she said softly as they walked down the hall, "were you born in Greeley?"

"Oh, my goodness no," the doctor said. "I was born in Prague, right before the war."

"Oh…." Danielle said, swallowing. "When did your family come here?"

"They did not come here," she said. "I came here when I was 20. My mother and father did not make it out of Czechoslovakia alive. Like so many, they did not. All I have left of them is the picture of me and my mother, and the piano playing that she taught me."

"How did you escape?" Danielle asked.

"We had a cleaning lady who lived outside of Prague. I used to go with her to her family's house in the country. My mother paid for me to go live with them. Nearby was a very small town with a lot of farmers and workers, and they didn't care that I was a Jewish doctor's daughter or a concert pianist's daughter. They just had me with their children. Safe."

The pianist smiled when she entered her room. "It smells clean," she said. Then she turned to Maria who was just coming out of the bathroom. "¿Para cuando espera a su bebé?"

The girl looked up with a face mixed with surprise and fear. She shook her head.

"¿Para cuando espera a su bebé?" The doctor repeated severely. "I know you're pregnant."

"Diciembre," Maria whispered.

The doctor nodded. "¿Dónde trabaja su esposo?"

"ColBeef."

"Bien," she said. "Danielle and Maria—you are both good workers and help me a great deal. Muchas gracias. Buenos noche."

The two young women left the room together.

"Danielle," the young woman spoke her name hesitantly. "Por favor… Please…say nothing about mi bebe."

Danielle shook her head. "No, of course not."

Then the girl who came up to about Danielle's shoulder gave her a quick hug. "I do the bathrooms today," she said. With a smile she hurried off.

The fall went fast. Danielle didn't register for any classes but started spending afternoons at the University of Northern Colorado's library. In the library, it seemed a long ways from the nursing home, the smell of the ColBeef meat packing plant, and Carl.

Carl himself was not at home that much. He and a bunch of other retired workers were now protesting at various street corners. His sign read "Give Jobs to real Americans---Enforse Immigration Laws now."

It made Danielle smile when she saw his misspelled sign. Dorothy just shook her head.

One morning in early November Dr. Kabisky looked at the two rather crossly. "Before you start my room today," she said, "I want to speak to Anahi. Danielle, please find her."

Danielle hurried to find the supervisor. "The doctor wants to see you," she said to Anahi, who was stocking a cart with cleaning supplies.

"About what?" she asked frowning.

"I don't know."

The woman closed her eyes and pursed her lips and they walked back quickly.

"Anahi," the doctor said, "it is unacceptable to have this young woman in her condition working with that heavy floor buffer. She cannot do that anymore. I saw her this evening, and it is not right."

"Alright," she said slowly, looking over Maria's body.

"Furthermore, I would like not to see her have to reach or bend as much as she normally does. What can you find her to do for the next month that will not hurt her or the child?"

"I'll have her sort silverware and laundry." Anahi was irritated but did not let her voice betray her feelings.

"No lifting heavy baskets," Dr. Kabisky warned.

"I'll have her to do socks."

Marie looked worried and said something very fast in Spanish.

"She never said anything to me," the doctor said, "but my eyes are not so bad that I cannot see that she's dropped already."

Anahi took a deep breath. "Alright. Anything else, Doctor?"

"No but don't give the girls a bad time about this. Don't make Danielle pick up the rest of the load. I notice that Pam seems to have plenty of time to sneak smokes so perhaps a little more on her plate is in order. Just not in my room."

Anahi's eyes rolled, but she said nothing. She scratched her head. Finally she said, "Thank you, Doctor. If there's nothing else, I'll go back to work.

"And I'll go practice my Chopin."

The two walked out together.

Being assigned the floor buffing did not go well with Pam. "If I wasn't so tired, I'd be joining those protesters downtown," she said to Danielle one evening as she came in from her smoke.

The protesters finally made it to the big time when Charlie Duffy, an obnoxious talk show host, broadcasted from the front of the Weld County Courthouse as Danielle drove home in the morning.

"Send these people to jail," he hollered into the microphone and into the kitchens of many Greeley residents. "If you send them home, they'll just come back. Put them where they can't bother us and take our jobs."

That night Anahi came looking for Maria at the beginning of the shift. The two talked in hushed voices outside of Dr. Kabisky's room. The only phrase that Danielle picked up was muy peligrosos. What was so dangerous?

The next morning when she came home Carl had the TV blasting. "We did it! The county raided ColBeef and arrested fifteen illegals. They're in jail now," he said triumphantly to Danielle.

The reporter on the TV asked a sheriff's official if this would be the end of the arrests. "No, we think some spouses are also in the community. We'll be looking for them as well."

Danielle got a phone call at noon from Theresa. "I know you just got off," she said. "But eight people didn't show up today to work in the kitchen and on the floor. Can you come in and cover a shift?"

Danielle was tired but thought it was better than hanging in the house with Carl and his friends who were celebrating the raid at ColBeef's.

"Hey, sweetie," Dorothy greeted as she got there. "Theresa is having me help anyone who hasn't worked on the floor. Your job will be to take the juice around this afternoon."

The place was crazy. There were three sheriff deputies on the floor and another law supervisor in an expensive overcoat. "It's about time you showed up," Dr. Kabisky was talking in a tone of voice that Danielle had never heard. "I called down to your office a week ago to report a theft."

"I am sorry, Dr. Kabisky," the man in the overcoat said. "I haven't heard anything about that."

"Well, I talked to someone but I can't say that I wrote their name down. He assured me someone would come out to talk to me about it," she said.

"What was stolen, ma'am?"

"I am a Doctor," she said "A ma'am is short for madam, and madam sounds as if I am running a brothel. Do you understand?"

"Yes," and he almost said ma'am again. "What was taken?"

"The diamond ring that was my mother's. I don't need you to investigate it. It was that girl—that girl Maria who works the night shift."

"Maria doesn't work here anymore," Theresa said. "Anahi fired her last week."

Danielle nearly dropped the glass of juice she was holding.

"Of course, she fired her the night I reported the missing ring. That's when it left the building."

Danielle felt shocked and almost said something, but Doctor Kabisky looked straight at her with a bit of a smile. "Now this girl is a hard worker. It must have happened when she was coming to get me from playing the piano. But that other one? Lazy and fat!"

Danielle thought she must be dreaming. Maybe she wasn't even at work. Maybe she was in bed and she needed to wake up.

"Well," the overcoat man said, "she's probably left the county. Her husband's one of the fifteen in jail. But we've haven't caught any of the spouses that worked here or elsewhere."

"No, they all heard news of the raid and didn't show up today. I got one big mess on my hands," Theresa said.

"You think you do? St. Pat's was having a roofing problem, and they had a bunch working up on that. They're all gone too. They'll be lucky if they have Christmas Eve service if they don't get that roof fixed."

"Well, enough about them. I want to know what you're going to do about that," Dr. Kabisky paused, looking at the sheriff and then with great bitterness said, "that Mexican that took my ring?"

"Doctor, I don't think I can do anything."

"Well, Ms. Hansen," she said, turning to Theresa, "I am not happy. Until I am comfortable with this situation, the only people to go into my quarters are Danielle and Anahi. Do I make myself clear?"

Theresa looked a little stunned. "Of course, Dr. Kabisky. I am sorry this has you so upset."

"You'd be upset if it was your mother's ring. Your mother who died in a concentration camp."

The older woman turned and walked into her room and shut the door.

"Danielle," Theresa said softly, "in a little bit, take a pot of tea and cake for Dr. Kabisky. I'd let her cool off a bit though first."

The manager and the sheriff staff walked further down the hall.

"So I take it you don't have any of the illegals here today," the sheriff said quietly.

"Not a one," Theresa said. "Some that were legal left. They all worked last night but I noticed their personal things are gone as well. It's really left me in a big mess."

"Hey, it's not my choice," the overcoat man said. "I have better things to do than to try to raid a nursing home."

"Could I interest you in changing a colostomy bag?" she asked. He laughed and then walked away.

Danielle went back after a short time with the pot of tea. She knocked first and heard music playing as she walked in. Classical, of course. There in the rocking chair was Maria with Dr. Kabisky sitting in an easy chair close by.

"Shh," the doctor said before Danielle could say anything.

"Oh," Danielle said with a sigh of relief. "I thought you were horrible out there. I thought maybe I was dreaming."

"Ahh…." the doctor said sweetly. "I was in a play in college and the director told me to stick to science. So I was convincing, yes?"

"Very much so," she said. Maria was smiling.

"And you frightened me," Danielle said.

"Ahh…perhaps I could become an actress next. So here's the situation," Dr. Kabisky said. "I heard Anahi and Maria talking last night. They seemed to forget that I spoke Spanish to many of my patients. It made them much more comfortable than trying to understand my English. So I reminded them that Maria is going to have a baby and she did not need to be bouncing around in a police car with all the other poor souls. Since Theresa doesn't look at timesheets until payday, Anahi tore Maria's up. I invited Maria to stay in my room at least until the baby comes or we figure out what to do next." The doctor took a breath and then smiled broadly.

"We will make use of the time as best as we can. I am teaching Maria some English. Could you please pick up some picture book for me in the library that I can use? Bilingual books would also be good."

Danielle did what she was instructed and for the next two weeks also brought extra food to the room. Anahi found out that Maria's husband, Joaquin, was still in Greeley in the county jail, along with now twenty-seven other men. Most were like him; they had come to Colorado as young men to find something better than the drug trade. Maria had only been in Colorado ten months when all of this came about. She was worried about her husband which made the doctor worry about her.

The two roommates got along fine. Soon they were playing cards, with Maria saying out loud in English the numbers as she laid them down. Three of diamonds, queen of hearts, rummy.

The tension in the city was high. Since it was so close to the holidays, Theresa did not want to hire new staff so everyone was working extra hard. There weren't many extra people to hire. Other places had the same situation—restaurants had school kids washing dishes with a lot of dishes still left unclean.

"There's still no reason for people to come over illegally," Pam said, "but I miss having the others here to help. Why doesn't Theresa hire extra people?"

"Now the administration thinks we can save some money until the end of the year. Finish out with a bigger profit," Anahi said as she mopped the floor outside of Dr. Kabisky room.

"What are they—a bunch of dirty, money-hungry Jews?"

Right then Dr. Kabisky came out. "You called?" she asked Pam who, red-faced, hurried away.

That night when Danielle came to clean Dr. Kabisky room, Maria was sleeping in the recliner. When Dr. Kabisky wasn't in the room, Maria usually hid in the closet, just in case. "Just leave her," Dr. Kabisky whispered. "It's a quiet evening."

They walked down the hall together. As she walked, the doctor rolled her neck and shoulders. "You are tired too," Danielle said.

"Yes, it's not as easy to sleep for me now when I wonder what will happen to Maria and the baby. But I'll play some Brahms' lullabies, and that will calm me."

Danielle hurried back to clean but Mr. Liepold from the other wing wandered over to the assisted living side so she had to take him back to his room and let the night nurse know to keep an eye on him. When she came around the corner, she saw Pam with her hand on Dr. Kabisky's door.

"No!" Danielle yelled. "You can't go in there."

She was shocked at how loud she sounded. Three residents poked their heads out.

"I was just going to straighten up in there," Pam said. "I saw you were busy."

Anahi came around the corner. "Mr. Thompson, you buzzed me. What are you doing out here? What's going on?" she said. "What's everyone doing up?"

"That woman was going into the doctor's room," Millie said helpfully. "Danielle stopped her."

"Pam, what were you doing?" Anahi looked worried.

"I said I was helping clean. Nothing to it."

"Go to the lounge and wait for me," the supervisor said. "I'll be there shortly." Pam turned and left.

"Now everyone, it's late. You need to get back to bed."

"Oh, we will. We just didn't want her to find out about Maria," Millie said.

Danielle and Anahi looked shocked. "We may be old," Ben Thompson added, "but we know what's going on. You and the doctor are not the only ones who speak Spanish."

"I see," Anahi said stiffly. "Please, everyone back to bed. Danielle, clean the room as quickly as possible."

So despite already having a staff shortage, Pam was fired that night. "I couldn't have her being so insubordinate," Anahi explained to Theresa.

"Not to Dr. Kabisky." Theresa nodded in agreement. "She just donated another $10,000 to our new wing fund."

Dorothy was working as much as Danielle. At this time of year Dorothy normally spent her time off cleaning and decorating the house for Christmas, but her enthusiasm changed when she found out that Cassie was going to her boyfriend's. "We couldn't afford to fly her back," she told Dr. Kabisky one day when they were talking. "Her financial aid has been cut back, and we barely cover it as it is, even with all my overtime. But it doesn't feel like Christmas without her coming home."

"Perhaps she can come for the New Year," the doctor said, "or Epiphany."

"Not this year. But we at least have Danielle. Carl is pretty down in the dumps about his daughter not being home at all, but it could be worse. I feel so sorry for all those families broken up by that stupid raid," Dorothy said.

"It is a hard time," Dr. Kabisky said. "When the war was going on, my father wanted me to go with the family very badly, but he cried when I left. I think he knew he wouldn't see me again."

"That family that took you in, were they Jewish too?" Dorothy asked, making reference to her religion for the first time in history.

"Oh no, they were good Catholics. I was raised Catholic when I was with them. No, they did what they did because there was an obligation. My father operated on their daughter who was my age when they had no money. That was why Virda worked for us. Father wasn't going to do the surgery, but my mother said, 'What if it was Hanna? What would you want someone to do?' She was the one who convinced my father to do the surgery. Then Virda was the one who made her husband take me in."

Dorothy smiled. "Carl's that way. He said we couldn't afford to help Danielle. But I said 'What if it was Cassie?' That was how we invited her back to live with us."

"Men aren't always as good as they could be," Dr. Kabisky laughed. "Maybe that's why the song says 'Peace on Earth, Good Will to Men'. We're praying that men get some good will."

"What would you like to hear tonight," Dr. Kabisky asked Danielle when they walked down to the piano.

"Could you play *What Child is This?*" she asked. "I loved singing that growing up."

"No, a Jewish pianist doesn't play that, but I can give you *Greensleeves*." The two laughed as she played the same melody as the Christmas carol. Danielle sang a verse as she headed to her cleaning.

The next day the doctor went to see the director of the nursing home.

"Ms. Hansen," Dr. Kabisky stood at the doorway.

"Yes, Doctor," Theresa said, wondering what brought the doctor to her office.

"I have a proposal," she said. "May I come in?"

Half an hour later, Kathy, Theresa's secretary, was copying off the invitation that went to all staff and residents.

Open House December 23
Sorry for the late notice, but you and your loved
ones are invited to an open house
Sunday, 2 p.m. December 23, sponsored by Dr. Kabisky.
There will be music, food and beverage, and a
special little gift from our dear doctor.
Hope you can come.

The unwritten message that Kathy passed onto every staff member was that Theresa hoped every staff member could make it as well as their spouse. The chances for a bonus increased dramatically for those in attendance.

The dining room was full the afternoon of the reception. The staff's families sat at their individual tables with cookies, cheese, and fruit. "Dorothy," Anahi said when they had sat down, "I am sorry to bother you, but could you come with me?" The two left together right when the doctor came in and stood in front of everyone.

"I know it is not unusual for me to play some music, but today I think you find my selection to be particularly entertaining," she said, sitting at the piano bench.

With that she launched into a rousing *It's Beginning to Look a Lot like Christmas*, followed by *Up on the House Top*. Then she got more religious, playing things like *Angels We have Heard on High*, and then *O Come All Ye Faithful*. For almost an hour she played one Christmas carol after another. The group loved it.

"Now, I hope I won't embarrass her, but I would like to invite Danielle to sing *Silent Night*," the good doctor said, beckoning Danielle forward. The audience clapped loudly and up she went.

While she was singing, Danielle saw Anahi standing in the doorway while Dorothy walked back to Carl's table. When Dr. Kabisky looked up, Anahi nodded. And the doctor nodded again. On the last verse everyone joined in, including her uncle, holding his wife's hand. Danielle remembered the last time she sang the song, standing in the Pershing Community Church, her dad's voice next to hers.

When they were done, there was a momentary pause, and then the whole room exploded in applause. Dr. Kabisky stood up, and bowed her head and then turned to Danielle, with outstretched arm. The place applauded even louder.

"Thank you all," the doctor said when it had quieted. "I wish you a blessed season and hope that this year brings you peace on earth." Danielle went back to her table and Dr. Kabisky with Theresa walked around to all the tables.

When they came to Danielle's table, Carl stood up. "Do you remember me?" he asked the doctor.

"Yes, I remember all my patients. Your eye has kept working all these years?"

"Yup, maybe I should have had you operate on my back."

The doctor laughed. "I don't know that I could have done anything with that," she said.

Dorothy spoke up. "It meant a lot you doing that surgery. And letting us pay for it gradually."

The doctor nodded. "I wonder if there's something you can do for me," she said quietly.

"Anything," Carl said. "Name it, Doc."

"Not here, but come to my room, and we'll discuss it."

Danielle looked at her aunt quizzically. "We're almost ready to leave," Dorothy said. "We'll stop by on the way out."

"Wonderful."

They ate a few more cookies. Carl talked to a couple of men on staff and then they looked in their envelopes. Both had gotten $50.

"Whooo...." Carl said. "That's something. Dr. Kabisky must have money up her ying yang."

"Carl...." The two women said in unison. He smiled.

The hall was still pretty quiet when they walked down it. "What do you suppose she wants?" Carl asked.

"You'll find out," Dorothy said. She gently knocked on the door.

"Come in," Dr. Kabisky said.

There in the rocking chair was Maria holding a baby. "When did the baby come?" Danielle cried.

"Shh….This morning at four," Anahi said, closing the door behind them. "The doctor and I delivered her. Maria didn't make a sound. She was an angel."

Maria was in a heavy coat. She looked exhausted. Next to her was a duffle bag, and bundles of diapers, and a car seat.

"What the…" Carl said loudly.

"Shh," Dorothy hushed him.

"We want you to take a bit of a trip," Dr. Kabisky said.

"We?" Carl looked confused.

"Yes, all of us," Dorothy said. "I've packed some clothes for you. And if you don't do it, I will."

"Do what exactly?"

"Get this young mother back to her family. You're driving as far as McAllen, Texas. She has family there who can get her back to her town in Mexico. She'll live there for a while and figure things out."

"Why would I help an illegal?"

"Because I helped you," Dr. Kabisky said, her grey eyes alight with fire. "I was there when you needed an eye surgeon."

"But what you're asking is illegal.

"It was illegal for the family that took me in back in the thirties. If they hadn't, Carl, I wouldn't have been in Greeley to save your eye. What is morally wrong about this young woman and her baby going back to Mexico where she will have family to love her and her baby and not worry about being put in jail?"

"Carl, what if it was Cassie? What if the shoe was on the other foot? What if it was Cassie who had a baby and they wouldn't let her come home to us?" Dorothy pleaded.

"It's still illegal," he insisted.

"Carl," Dr. Kabisky said, but then Dorothy spoke up louder—in a tone Danielle had never heard.

"Carl, I have been with you for 24 years. I've put up with you through sickness and health. I have never asked much of you, but I want you to take this girl to Texas. If you don't, I will."

"And there's a bit extra for you, once she's home safe," Dr. Kabisky said. She ripped out a check. "It's made out to Dorothy just so that I know you do what I ask."

He looked at the check made out for two thousand dollars. The man sighed.

"I don't know what to say," he said.

"Say yes," Dr. Kabisky said. "If you leave now, there will be time for you to celebrate and Cassie will be coming home to you on Epiphany."

He looked at his wife whose eyes were shiny with tears, but also strong with determination. "The doctor gave me some money for a ticket. She'll be able to get back by the 6th of January," Dorothy said. Carl's eyes became shiny, then he looked down and finally he looked at the young woman holding the baby.

"Alright," he said. "Let's get moving."

Dr. Kabisky nodded her head. "I'd like to hold the baby one more time, if that's alright?" she said. Maria nodded, handing the little girl over to the old woman. "Have you decided on her name? ¿Como se llama?"

Maria smiled. "Se llama …Hanna Anahi."

"Ahh….we'll be the fairy Godmothers," Dr. Kabisky said with a smile. She gave the baby a small kiss on the forehead. "God bless you both," she said, "and you too, Carl."

Dorothy and Danielle worked all Christmas Eve and Christmas Day. Carl returned home the morning of December 26th. They celebrated

Christmas that year on the 6th of January when Cassie came home for the long weekend.

Danielle never saw Maria and Hanna Anahi again, but in April Dr. Kabisky got a picture from Mexico with the young woman holding a beautiful baby. She put it on the shelf alongside the picture of her mother holding her. Every December a new one arrived. She kept each picture up on the shelf until the year she died.

Waiting for Michael

The Rocky Mountains were beautiful as Brittany looked west from the parking lot. Fresh snow rested on the gray foothills that crisp November morning. It was probably good skiing at Keystone and A-Basin ski resorts, but Brittany had not even hit the slopes yet this season. She sighed, lowered her gaze to the red brick buildings beyond a twelve foot barb-wired fence keeping the boys at the Clear Mountain Detention Center away from the rest of Denver.

The 19-year-old dreaded this visit. This was the first of her three observations with the Silas' Place program at Clear Mountain, part of the Intro to Counseling class she had gotten stuck with when she couldn't get the psychology class she wanted. If she had known it required going to places like this to see what the facilities were like, she would have found something else, even if it had been a 7:30 a.m. gym class.

She registered for it the day her dad made her mad most recently. He and his latest girlfriend, Mindy or Lindy, had taken her out for lunch. It should have been just her dad and Brittany. So when Mindy/Lindy asked her what she was majoring in, Brittany had answered sociology just to piss him off. Now she was paying the price.

It had been fun to see him spit and sputter in the restaurant. "You're going to be a counselor? Do you know what those people earn?" he asked. "You're going to the University of Denver which costs for one year what those people are lucky to make after five years of work. Are you nuts?"

"Not everybody wants to crunch numbers or make people buy things they don't need," she shot back.

"Really?" he said. "You seem to enjoy buying $70 jeans or a pair of $250 ski boots you don't need, thanks to my number crunching." She couldn't think of anything snarky to shoot back at him so she glared at him and the girlfriend the rest of the lunch. It was a good thing that she had spent Thanksgiving with her mom instead of him and Mindy/Lindy. Now she had to get through this semester and Christmas day with him.

The intro counseling course required the students visit three different facilities on three different occasions. She had visited the Good Angels' Center—a home for elderly with dementia. Her grandmother was in a place like this in Minnesota and she hoped no angels smelled like that place.

At St. Luke's Hospice there had been lots of crying. Thank God, no one she had sat with had died while she was there. That would have been so gross.

Her mom kept asking her what she was learning in the class. Her answer was always the same. "I am learning that there's no way in hell I am going to be a counselor."

Her mother had been a social worker before children but had stayed home when Brittany and her brother Brent were little. Now after the divorce, her mother was trying to find work again in the field and was talking of going back to school. *Well, she could have the joy of being with people who drooled and stared off into space when you tried to talk to them. Maybe being around those sad people would make her feel a little better about her life.*

All in all, her mom's life wasn't so bad. She had kept the house because Brent was still at home. Her dad was pretty generous with the money too so Mom wasn't forced to go find a job immediately. Dad was paying for Brittany's college, her apartment, and a good allowance as well. Yet it still sucked that after twenty-two years of marriage, they had split up. Mom was talking about finding something to do. *What I want to do is find a way out of this class.* It wasn't going to happen because she waited too long to drop it without paying for it, and her dad would have a fit if he found out. A number cruncher pays attention to those things.

At least maybe this place wouldn't smell. This place dealt with young men who had done bad things, sometimes very bad things, but who probably didn't have to wear Depends. Some acts she had read about in the Denver Post as part of her orientation to knowing what she was getting into. Her dad was so right that she'd be better off in business.

"Your time," Mr. Carver, the main counselor at Silas' Place, said over the phone, "will not be directly with the detainees. I hope that's alright."

There is a God. "What will I be observing?"

"Who not what." He seemed irritated about something. "Our program deals with the families. You'll meet them and deal with them. You need to be there for them. It can be hard. They feel guilt, anger, sadness. You name it, and they feel it."

She had noticed that he had used the word 'deal' instead of 'observe'. "So I'll be observing the families at Clear Mount like I did at St. John's?"

"Kind of except some here have hope that their kid will still turn out alright. Along with the fear that they won't. There is much more an unknown outcome as opposed to St. John's."

Ben Carver was in a hurry when he met her at the entrance the next week. "You're late," was how he greeted her. "Some will be here in fifteen minutes." He was a bear of a man, with a balding head, and a belly that folded over his belt several inches even though he was in his early thirties. His shirt was sweat stained despite the forty degree temperature outside.

"Let me show you where you'll work." Once again, Brittany heard the word 'work' instead of the safe, passive tone that 'observe' conveyed. He took her through the first series of gates, each locked and with a camera above it.

"Ok. Families have different ideas on how long their children may be here than the court has for their sons. We strongly urge them to go through counseling so they know what their son is going through while they're here. Some might come in to talk about what they'll do when their son comes home. If their son isn't coming home in the near future, the parents become resigned or depressed. Some even need counseling just to be able to meet their son under these conditions." He led her into a small room, with a worn couch, and a coffee table, and a few old magazines from 2012.

"Here's Donna Hammen," he said, nodding to the woman sitting behind a desk. "She's our hostess with the mostest."

A tall, too-thin woman stood up. Her hair was long and pulled back into a ponytail. *Women her age shouldn't wear a ponytail or skip the makeup.* Brittany worked an hour each morning to look natural and most people said she was cute, with her short punky blonde cut with little red streaks.

"Hello Brittany," she said. "Welcome to Clear Mount. How are you doing?"

"Thanks Donna," Brittany said. "I'm a little nervous."

"Oh, you're perfectly safe up here," Ben said, eyeing the five foot-two woman. "Nobody can get you."

"No, it's not that," Brittany said. "I guess I was under the impression I would observe, not do anything here."

"Really? That's not what Dr. Adams said. He said I could put you students to work," Ben said absentmindedly as he looked through a pile of papers.

"I am just not sure what I am getting into. What will the families want or say?"

"They'll say 'my son's innocent'. Or it was the girlfriend's fault or 'what's my baby going through' and ten million other things," Donna said. "And you'll listen politely sometimes, and you'll get mad at other times."

"That's about right," Ben said. "Donna knows better than I do what they'll say."

"I've just been here longer," the woman said with a smile. "Let me show you the counseling room."

The room had a round table and a picture of Jesus with a flock of sheep. There was a Bible as well a cross on the bookcase. On Donna's desk had been a small crèche.

"Why so religious?" Brittany asked, feeling more out of place than ever in this strange place.

"We're a faith based organization even if we are in a public facility. They allow us the room, but don't pay us," Ben answered.

"Does that seem ethical? I mean, separation of state and religion," she asked. She was also studying constitutional law this semester. In that class there was always something that she could tell her mom that she had learned. *Maybe law instead of business.*

"I take away everything after we're done," he responded, "except for the hope. That's what I try to give them. Because you need to give them hope of some sort," Ben said, "even if they never get through it."

The first visitor that day was a large sloppily dressed woman with missing teeth called Alma Fisher. "Mrs. Fisher," Ben said gently, "thank you for coming."

"Not sure why I am here," she said. "I don't have so much time that I can spend it riding two buses over here and then going through this bullshit. I'd just like to shake Xandu until his teeth fall out."

"Your son," Ben started to say.

"My grandson," Mrs. Fisher said. "His goddamn mother left him on my doorstep, and I don't know where the hell she is. All she's ever given him is that God-awful name."

"Your grandson is fourteen," Ben said.

"Fourteen—going on twenty-one," she said still angry. "He's been hanging out with his cousins who are older. They're the ones who got him into this trouble—those gangbangers."

"So he was driving a car," Ben said.

"Yeah, he didn't know they were going to hold up that liquor store," she said starting to tear up. "I thought he was playing basketball over at the Boys and Girls Club."

"At midnight?" Ben asked.

"I can't keep track of him. I've got to be at my job at the hospital by six a.m. I am not going to wait up for him."

"So how many years," Brittany asked, "will he be here?"

"Just four; he'll get out when he's eighteen. Then I hope he'll join the army. Maybe that will straighten him out."

"So why are you here?" Ben asked.

"I am here," she said softening just a bit, "because I want him to get through this. His uncle, my Billy….he didn't make it. He got out and then back in and then out and back in…and then one day some white supremacist asshole stabbed him at the state pen. I don't want that for

Xandu. But I don't know what to do except pray for him, and that didn't work so well the last time."

Then the stone-faced woman broke down and wept hard. Brittany felt utterly helpless until Ben broke through the tears. "Brittany," Ben said, "why don't you see if there's some coffee for Mrs. Fisher?"

She was glad to escape. "How's it going?" Donna asked softly, looking up from a pile of papers she was sorting.

"I don't know what to do in there," she replied.

"You're listening, right?" Donna said. "That's what Mrs. Fisher needs today."

Brittany took the coffee and the tray of sugar and fake milk in and by that time Ben had Mrs. Fisher calm again. "So what you'll want to do is to talk to him about something he's close to and that brings out the soft side."

"He loves his niece," she said. "He calls her Lil Bug. She's only four."

"Then bring pictures of her, and maybe some drawings she's done. The soft side will take over the hardness in his heart."

"Won't that make him..?" she started to say and then stopped.

"Vulnerable?" he said, then seeing that she didn't understand he added, "too easy to be taken advantage of?"

"Yeah, he's not that big." Her voice was breaking again.

He shrugged. "Vulnerable can make him stronger—to get through this for a reason. He needs a reason to change in here. That there's something better on the outside."

They talked for a few minutes and she then said, "I'll come back Sunday and see him, if that's alright." The woman looked slightly hopeful.

"I think it will be," Ben said, opening the door. "Wait a minute." He called out to Donna, "Is Pod B headed to the gym right now?"

"Looks like it," she said, peering out of the blinds.

"Ok, Mrs. Fisher," he said. "Your kid's pod is outside right now."

A group of boys were walking outside in the cold in their orange jump suits. She rushed to the window.

"There he is," she said pointing to a kid at the back. "That's Xandu."

"He is a handsome young man," Donna said.

"Oh, he is," she said proudly. "Why don't he have a coat on? It's freezing."

"Mrs. Fisher, they don't wear coats just to go to the gym," Ben said. "Besides he probably never wore a coat at home, did he?"

"No. He'd freeze his ass off before he'd wear a coat." She smiled for the first time that day. "Thank you for your help."

She left the room. "Merry Christmas," Donna called out.

A redheaded lady with two little boys was sitting nervously in the reception area. "Ms. Green," Ben said, "won't you come in?"

That day they must have seen twelve women, varying ages and races, not one man in the bunch. Some were mad; some were sad. Through it all Brittany watched Ben talk to the women, then listen to their anger and tears. She watched Donna hug or gently touch each woman as they came in, bringing in coffee and tissue when it was needed. Donna gave them information sheets. She sat and listened to them while they were waiting for their turn.

Only at one point was Donna ever gone from the room. The phone was ringing. "Go pick that up," Ben said. "1:30 is when Donna takes a break."

Brittany went out to get the call and was surprised to see Donna standing by the window, just looking out. Brittany picked up the phone and said "Silas' Place, Brittany speaking."

She listened for a minute and then said, "I don't know. Let me ask." She covered the receiver and whispered loudly. "Donna, there's a woman on the phone who wants to know if she can come on Thursday instead of today. Something about her babysitter didn't show up."

The woman by the window did not say anything. "Donna," she said louder. Then Donna held up her hand with one finger. After a few seconds she sighed and turned to Brittany, taking the phone from her.

"This is Donna." Her voice was almost a whisper. "Ok," she said. "Let me see what I can do. Give me your number and I'll call you back."

"Sorry," she said to Brittany. "I was thinking about something." Her eyes looked shiny, but then she smiled. "Look at you," she said to the heavyset woman walking in. "You've lost some weight. You're looking good, Patty."

"Thanks, Donna. I am working out four days a week. I wanted to let you know that Justin's appeal has been scheduled for another hearing. He may be let out."

"That's wonderful," Donna said, "but you'll still have an adjustment to make."

"I know. He's not the perfect little angel that I thought he was." The woman named Patty smiled. "And I am not going to let him slide, just because his dad isn't around."

"No, that isn't doing him any favors," Donna said. "And I know it isn't easy, but you're doing the right thing."

"It's hard, but I want him home for Christmas or at least by New Year's. How's your son?" she asked.

"Fine, as far as I know," Donna said, "but do you ever know?"

The two women hugged. "I just wanted to thank you," Patty said. "You've really helped me out this last year."

"My pleasure," Donna said, "but you've really helped yourself. Keep me posted and keep losing that weight."

They embraced again, and she went out the door. "Ben," Donna called out.

"What?" he asked, filling up another of cup of coffee and grabbing a cookie.

"Patty Abbott dropped in. Justin got his appeal."

"Oh boy," he said. "You think he'll get off this time?"

"Maybe," she said. "Legal technicality."

"I don't know whether that boy should be out again." He shook his head. "He's too smart for his own good."

"Patty's smarter too. I think it will be ok. She's just beaming."

"It's almost as good as giving birth."

"Almost as painful," Donna said. She started humming a little song as she went around picking up and cleaning the reception area while Ben put the religious items away.

"Well, what did you think of your first day?" Ben asked Brittany as he locked the door on the way out.

"I don't know what I am doing," she said. "Am I just to listen or am I just to give advice? I don't know what these women are going through."

"I don't either," he laughed. "I know if our son was locked up, my wife would be fighting like a tiger to get him out. But sometimes I think the women are relieved that their kid isn't on the street anymore."

"It's got to be hard," Brittany said lamely.

"Some say it's harder than having them die," Ben said. "I had a woman who had a kid killed in Iraq and another one in here. She said having the one in here was harder because she didn't know how it was going to turn out."

"How old are these kids?" she asked.

"The youngest we've got are ten years old. The oldest is eighteen; once they turn nineteen they're either released or go to an adult facility."

"That's horrible." She thought of her twelve-year-old brother being in a place like this. Brent was such a brat at times. He had gotten into big trouble with some graffiti when their dad left, acting real tough.

But he was still a kid. Being away from home would freak him out. He didn't even go to camp last year because he didn't want to be gone from his mother.

"They're not your typical ten-year-olds," he said, then added, "thank God. We had one kid who was killing and torturing the pets in the neighborhood, but no one knew who it was. Then he moved up and killed a five-year-old boy."

She shook at the thought. "I am surprised the families want to have anything to do with them."

"They're still their children," he said. "They still love them but I don't know how they do it."

Brittany wondered how any parent did anything. Maybe growing up, getting a job wasn't what it was meant to be. There was too much shit in these places. At the Hospice Center, there was sadness and nobody got better. At the Alzheimer's facility, there was a lot of smells and nobody got better. It seemed like this place no one knew if their kid would get better. She was sure that there had to be some place a social worker could work that didn't seem so sad or tragic. Maybe baby adoptions. Or maybe she'd go for business like Dad wanted her to. She looked at the University's program when she got back to her apartment and tried not to think of Brent being at Clear Mount.

The second week started out like her first until after 1:30. "I've got a meeting," Ben said. "Mrs. Wilson just got here, and Donna is on break. You talk to her."

"What will I say?" she said.

"Let me look at the file," he said quickly. "Ok, her son is 16. He's in here for setting buildings on fire. No one got hurt, but the potential was there. Here's a script. You can pretty much follow it."

He handed her a card that was pretty well worn, reading; "My name is..... How are you feeling today?"

78

The next questions dealt with what services to offer as well as an ending that suggested how to close the meeting with a prayer, a prayer that was provided.

Mrs. Wilson was a tiny woman, smaller than Brittany. "Hello, Mrs. Wilson," she said. "I am Brittany Parker. How are you today?"

"Not good. My boy Tommy is in here. He's really a good boy. I don't know if he did what they said or not." She spoke fast with an Asian accent that Brittany had trouble following.

"Do you think he could do this?"

The tiny woman shook. "I think so. I found fireworks in his room, and he always liked candles. I worried that he'd set the house on fire sometime when he would fall asleep."

"Do you have other children?" she said looking at the sheet.

"I have three but they're not like Tommy. They're good girls."

"How about his father? What does he think?"

"I don't know. He's a trucker so he away a lot," she said, tearing up. "He says, 'I bring in the money, you raise the kids.'"

"That sucks," she said automatically. Her dad used to say the same thing. He audited other locations of the company he worked for so that meant flying away for long weeks and exhausted over weekends.

"I don't know, that's the way my family was back in Vietnam. My husband's white and that's the way he was raised." She shrugged.

"How are your girls feeling?" she asked. *They feel like shit, just like I did when I knew that the neighbors knew what Brent had done.*

"They're ashamed. He was in their school and everyone knows. It's hard."

"We have counseling for them; in a group of kids their own ages, they can talk freely. There's a men's group too."

"They won't come," Mrs. Wilson said, closing her eyes. "Tommy's dad won't come either. It's my problem and Tommy's."

"Mrs. Wilson, would you like to say a prayer?" She wasn't sure what else to say.

"That would be nice," the small woman said.

"Keep Tommy safe and his mother strong," Brittany said stiffly, following the words on the card. "Help the days to go fast and help him gain what he needs before he leaves here. Help him remember that he is still loved by his family and his God. Amen."

The woman broke down and cried hard. "That was beautiful," she said finally through her tears. "Thank you for talking to me."

The petite woman looked a little stronger, despite the tears. "Is there anything else you'd like to talk about?" Brittany asked.

"I don't think so, but thank you for listening to me. I need someone to listen. I needed someone to care."

Brittany was shocked. Her dad always told her that she was pretty spoiled or that she should listen to what he had to say. Her mother suggested not talking as much in front of her dad. "I am glad," she said. "Are you sure there's not anything else I could do?"

The woman shook her head. "Merry Christmas," the woman said tearfully as she walked out the room.

I've done something good today. Brittany blinked in surprise.

But the third week started out badly. She left the apartment before eight only to find disaster in the parking lot. Her car—her little blue perfect Cooper— had a gash along its shiny side. Someone had keyed it all along the driver's side.

Son of a bitch. What asshole did this? She looked around hoping to see someone that she could blame and saw that the cars next to her had also been defaced. One even had a windshield smashed. It'd be the type of thing Brent would think was funny. Her car was special— her graduation gift from her dad or maybe his guilt payment. He left the spring of her senior year to move in with someone else before Lindy/

Mindy. That lasted through the summer, but her car looked great a year later.

"Dad, someone screwed up my car," she said into the cell phone, then telling him the details. She felt herself tearing up as she talked.

"Call the insurance company, honey. I don't have time to deal with it today. I am leaving for LA in an hour."

"But what do I do?" she asked.

"You're twenty years old. Call the insurance agent and let him know. Call your mother. I got to go."

The phone beeped into silence. Brittany glared up at the sky. "I'm nineteen, jerk," she said to no one.

That's what he had said when he told her about the divorce. "I got to go." She hated those words. She slammed the car door after she got the insurance card and made the call. What she wanted to hear was "I'll take care of it. I'll take care of you."

After waiting fifteen minutes on hold with her insurance company, she was told by someone that she needed a police report. The police took their goddamn time in getting out there.

"Not really going to pay to turn this in," the cop said. "You'll probably have a deductible."

"Yeah, but my car looks like shit now," she said still in a rage.

"I've seen worse," the cop said, shrugging. "Look around, there's some much worse than yours. But do what you want."

She was already running late and when she got to Silas' Place, the room was full of women. "Ben's not here," Donna explained. "You're on your own. I'll help whenever I can, but I have the front desk and this room full of women to deal with."

"Couldn't we just cancel today?" Brittany asked.

"No, there are too many women who took off work to be able to do this. Some drove hours to get here," Donna said with a smile. "You'll be fine. You did great with Mrs. Wilson last week. Just talk to them and listen. Here's the card that Ben made for these situations."

"I don't know why he's here," the first lady, Mrs. Thomas, said. "He's never done anything wrong."

"It sounds like he got caught stealing a car," Brittany said looking at the file.

"He wasn't stealing; he was borrowing it," Mrs. Thomas said angrily. "He needed to get to work. If he was such a bad boy, he wouldn't be working."

"Your job is to make him have something to look forward to when he comes home," she said, reading the card that Ben had provided for her.

"To look forward to? We've lost the house after I'd pay the lawyer and because I missed so much work. I don't care—the neighbors were talking about me anyway. His sisters and brothers won't have anything to do with him. They're so pissed off at him. What's it going to be like when he's home, wherever that ends up being?"

"I have no idea," Brittany said. "Would you like to pray?"

"Where was your god in the first place?" she said. "Keep your goddamn prayer."

No one else got as mad as Mrs. Thomas, but the morning was filled with women crying one after another, giving Brittany a headache. She went out once for a glass of water and saw Donna hugging a woman.

"Your son vandalized a commuter parking lot," Brittany said to Lenora Perry who was her fifth woman that morning. "He smashed 100 car windshields." Then she stopped reading from the card. "You think that's normal?"

"It's not normal, I know that," Lenora said. "He was just high that day and wanted to hear the noise."

"Cars matter," she said angrily. "People have to fix them. Then they don't have any way to get to work."

"I know. We'll try to make restitution. His father said he'll help."

"Restitution?" she said. "That's a joke. You can't make restitution for the time they had to make up for work to take care of their car."

Brittany was now as pissed as when she saw her car, but the woman sat there unaware of her rage. "I know he has to pay," Lenora said. "He's just been so upset since his dad left. He'll help us pay."

"Someone should pay," Brittany said angrily. *Dads leave all the time.* "Ok, so anything else you want to talk about?"

The answer was no and Brittany prayed the prayer with Mrs. Perry. She was starving and her head ached when she left the room at 1:35. *Maybe someone left donuts.* She walked into the empty reception area, quiet except for the phone ringing on the desk. Donna was looking out the window.

"Silas' Place. Brittany speaking. No, he isn't in today. Ok." She hung up the phone, hard.

"You know, I know you're a volunteer," she said to Donna as she walked over to the window. "I know that you take break at 1:30. But I am only an intern and I am starving. The goddamn phone was ringing. Couldn't you get it?"

"No," she said without looking at the young woman. "I am waiting for Michael."

"Who the hell is Michael?" Brittany demanded.

"My son," Donna said, looking briefly at Brittan and then back out the window. "Every day, he goes from Pod B to the gymnasium at 1:30. That's when I see him. That's when I know he's alright. But today I didn't see him." The calm Donna started shaking so violently that she had to sit down.

"What's the matter?" Brittany said. "What are you talking about?"

"He's not there today," the woman said. "I don't know where he is."

"He's here at Clear Mount?" Brittany asked dumbly.

"Yes. Every day I watch for him, except on Saturday and then on Sunday I visit here. Last week he said someone was mad at him. He thought maybe this guy would get some of the other guys and beat him up."

"He's probably fine," she said. "Maybe he has a cold."

"You don't miss gym if you have a cold. I think maybe they got him." She started shaking.

The phone rang again. Donna stood there and then bolted to the restroom. Somehow Brittany answered, "Silas' Place. Can I take a message?" Three other women came in and Brittany offered them coffee. "I am sorry. Ben isn't here today, but if you'd like to talk with me, I am here."

The rest of the afternoon flew by. Thank God, it was her last day. She had three finals, and she was free for the semester. She thought ahead. Sleeping through the weekend and skiing on Monday when everybody had to go to work. It was going to be heaven compared to this place.

At four Donna came in, still red-nosed, but with a faint smile. "Brittany," she said slowly, "I had a call from Ben."

There was a long pause and finally Brittany said, "Ok?"

The woman looked at her. "He wondered if you would do him a favor," she said hesitantly.

"What kind of favor?"

"He's going to need next week off," she said. "His wife is having a baby and there were complications today. She's in the hospital now, but they've ordered bed rest for her after she's released." Donna took a long sigh and smiled at Brittany.

Brittany waited for the woman to continue. "He has some people covering for him the rest of this week, but then there's nobody for Monday next week." Donna smiled at her again.

"Is he nuts?"

"I asked him the same thing but at this time of year it's impossible to get anyone else in, too much with travelling home for Christmas. If you want, you can sit at the front desk, and I'll talk to folks like Ben does and you did today."

"But I am out of school," she said.

"I know," the woman nodded, "but I can't do this by myself. If we don't keep it open, it's really hard on the mothers. You saw what a mess I was."

"But I was going to go skiing," she said. "I was going to be with my friends."

"Brittany," Donna said sternly, "you can go skiing when Ben gets back. Please, I am asking you to do this, and it's not easy for me to do so."

"I don't want to wait to go skiing. I don't know these women. I don't really care that their kids are all screwed up." She felt angry, like a child denied her favorite toy. She'd put in her time, damn it! She couldn't give another second of her life to this place.

"Everyone is waiting for something," Donna said. "I am waiting for Michael. You're waiting to hit the slopes. These women are waiting for something too."

"They won't get it from me," she said.

"I think they can."

Brittany sucked in a breath, trying to calm herself. "But it scares me. I don't know what to tell them."

"We can do it. You and I can handle the women Monday." Donna was as stubborn as a dog barking at a squirrel.

"Alright," Brittany said, "but don't think I am going to be all cheerful and perky."

"Would never expect it," Donna said and Brittany bristled.

"I am going home now," she announced. "I have three finals Thursday and Friday."

"Good luck. You'll do fine." Donna went back to her desk.

She walked out the door. *I'm not going to go do it. I'll call and leave a message. Or I'll figure out her email. There's no way I am doing this.*

But the rest of the week Brittany was so busy studying for her tests that she forgot about it. Thursday night she went out with some friends after studying for the last final and then she overslept the next morning. She was rushing to class when she ran into a gray-haired man coming out of the building.

"Excuse me, Dr. Adams," she said when she saw it was the professor from the Intro to Counseling class.

"Brittany, nice to see you. I've heard good things about you and Silas' Place."

"You have?" she said surprised.

"Yeah, I have to admit, I thought it was really a mistake for you to go into counseling after I heard the report about you from the hospice. But this was more reassuring."

"I am not sure what you mean."

"Well, the hospice said you never connected with anyone and kept everyone at an arm's length. They didn't see you contributing, but Donna over at Clear Mount had nothing but good things to say about you."

"When did you talk to her?"

"On Monday morning. She told me you were helping out this next week as well. That's just great. Well, I've got to get to my next class. Have a good Christmas."

"You too," she said.

She went in and for a moment thought about Donna. *Why on earth would she say that before she even asked me?* Brittany put the thought away and then aced the test.

Monday the snow came down the hardest of all season. The slopes would have been wonderful. Brittany showed up at Clear Mountain by 8:30, wondering if Donna would be there. "Donna said you were coming," the guard at the entrance said, smiling at her for the first time.

"Good. I was afraid she wouldn't be there."

"I don't think Donna has missed a day in three years, even when we've had blizzards and snow up to, well, you know."

"Makes for good skiing when it's that high."

"Too cold for me," he said with a smile. "Have a good day."

She wondered if he was the guy she had seen every single time she had come out here, never saying anything other than "I need to see your ID". She walked through the detection devices and up the stairs. "Hello," she called out when she didn't see anyone.

"Good morning!" Donna's voice was back to its normal cheerful self. "You came."

"Yeah, I kind of felt like I had to after Dr. Adams thanked me so profusely for agreeing to help."

"Oh, that. He called and wanted to know how you were doing, and I just thought he should know that you were coming back."

"Except you talked to him before you talked to me."

She laughed. "Oh, I knew you would say yes. Now let's look at who's coming today."

She pulled out a folder. "There are five or six first timers. These women need to go through this to be able to see their son over Christmas so that's why we're trying to get through this orientation."

The new women came in varying degrees of reaction. Ms. Harper was belligerent because the "goddamn attorney should have done a better job." Ms. Poltzi was crying and Brittany didn't know whether she spoke English or not through her tears. Ms. Callan was tired. The woman had driven from Grand Junction two hundred miles away to get there early so she could work her night shift when she got back home.

"I wished I understood," she said to Brittany. "He had everything—a nice house, a normal family, and seemed like he was doing fine. Then he killed that boy."

She felt her heart stop. "Your son killed someone?"

"Yeah," the mother said. "His best friend who started dating his girlfriend."

For a minute Brittany's mind flashbacked to Central High's Senior Prom when her date Evan had gotten drunk and punched out Peter Daniels when he thought Brittany and Peter were dancing too close. There was the moment after he had hit Peter that he looked at her as if he could kill her. Mr. Johnson, the science teacher, came over and broke it up, and she had called her mom to get her instead of staying at the dance. It had felt terrifying at the time. She broke up with Evan the next day. She heard later that he was arrested in a drug deal after high school and had beaten up the dealer bad.

She took a breath. This woman looked normal, like the mother of any of her friends.

"You want to see his picture?" Mrs. Callan asked, pulling out a billfold that had his school picture in it. "He was a junior last year. I am not sure whether he'll graduate or not now."

"Of course, he can graduate," Donna said, coming out of the counseling room. "He's a nice looking kid. Let's go talk about what you can do to help him," she said with her hand on the woman's arm, leading her into the office.

By the time Mrs. Callan left, it was snowing hard again. "Drive safely," Donna advised.

"She seemed so normal," Brittany said. "Her son looked like a nice kid."

"I think he probably is," Donna said. "It sounds like it was hormones and alcohol problems, and no one to talk to. One of those stupid things."

"A stupid thing that ended with him killing someone," Brittany said. "How does someone do that? Why do they do it?"

"I wish I knew. I mean there are kids who face the same thing that these kids do, and nothing happens." Her face suddenly paled. "What time is it," she asked.

It's 1:45," Brittany said.

"Oh damn it! I've missed Michael." The tears welled up in her eyes.

"I am sorry. Did you talk to him on Sunday?"

"I don't talk to him ever," Donna said. "I talk to Angel, his cellmate. He was the one who told me that someone had threatened him."

"Why don't you talk to Michael?" she asked.

"Because Michael doesn't want to see me," Donna said, her eyes closed against the tears. "He wishes I was dead."

Donna!" Brittany said feeling shocked. "I don't believe that. You're so nice."

"Brittany," she said taking a deep swallow, "my son tried to kill me. He killed his father and his sister. He doesn't want to talk to me."

The phone mercifully rang and Donna went to pick it up. "Silas' Place, Donna speaking," she said cheerfully as though nothing had happened.

Brittany felt like someone had punched her in the stomach. Then a woman with a walker came in. "I am here to see the counselor," she said. "My grandson is in here."

Donna turned and smiled and held up a finger, motioning for her to have a seat. "Would you like some coffee?" Brittany asked.

"That would be lovely," she said. "It's so cold out there today."

Donna finished her conversation and then came over with a tray of little Christmas cookies. "I am Donna," she said. "Would you like a cookie before we start our session?"

The two went in together as if they were old friends. Brittany wondered why a boy would kill his father and sister and try to kill his mother. She logged onto the computer which was slower than anything and googled Donna Hammen, Denver. There, three years ago, was a story about Michael Hammen, a 13-year-old boy who killed his father and sister as they slept. The mother had been attacked when she came up from letting the dog out and had managed to survive. Michael had pled guilty and was sentenced to Clear Mount.

"So now you know my story," Donna said, standing looking over Brittany's shoulder. "I am the survivor."

"I am so sorry," Brittany said. "I don't know what to say."

"Nobody does," Donna said. "Those who come closest are the other mothers of the murderers."

"Why?" she couldn't help asking.

"I ask that every day," Donna said. "I don't know why. Let's close this place up and get out of here." She picked up the cross and threw away the napkins and tissues on the table. She wiped off cookie crumbs into her hands.

Brittany watched the woman do the work that she must do every day. "Donna," she asked, "could we have a cup of coffee somewhere?"

"You mean you don't drink enough coffee when you're here?" The woman laughed.

"No, I just want to talk a little more," she said, "if it's alright."

"There's a Starbucks on the corner when you leave here. I'll see you there."

They arrived at the same time. "So what did you want to talk about?" Donna asked. "My life or yours?"

"I guess yours." Brittany's problems seemed trivial in comparison. "How do you, how do you go on every day with knowing that Michael killed your husband and daughter, and tried to kill you?"

"The clock radio goes off. I get out of bed and feed the dog. I run or do yoga and then I take a shower. Pretty exciting, huh?" She smiled sadly.

"Sounds pretty normal," Brittany said.

"I am normal. My family was normal. Except Michael one day went crazy."

"Did you see it coming?" she asked.

Donna shook her head. "One day he's yelling at us that he hates us; then that night he's cuddling on the couch with us. One minute he's using language like I have never heard before. Then the next minute he's telling me he loves me, especially my chocolate chip cookies. I thought this is what juvenile boys do."

"There must have been a sign," Brittany said. "Why would he do this?"

"You know, the investigators looked at everything. His attorney looked at everything. They checked to see if he was being abused; they checked his brain; they checked to see if he was performing witchcraft. That was almost as bad as being attacked."

"There was no reason?" Brittany asked. "Maybe he was doing drugs."

"There weren't any in his system," she said. "And you know it doesn't really matter. He killed John, my husband, and Cara, my daughter, and he tried to kill me. What kind of boy does that?"

"What he does say?"

"Oh, nothing to me. And the attorney says there's nothing to explain. He pled guilty and now he's here."

"How can you come out here?" she asked. "How can you be out here with these other mothers?"

"I didn't do anything for a while. I was in the hospital for three weeks after I got an infection in the wound. I didn't see him at the hearing. I was so angry." She took a small sip of her coffee and stared out the window at the snow on the road. Brittany felt like she should say something but nothing running through her head made any sense.

"Then one night," Donna said without looking at her, "I realized that he was all I had left. And that I still loved him. But he wouldn't see me so that was when I came to Silas' Place; I needed counseling myself. Then I started working out here, and that's what I've been doing ever since."

"Why doesn't he want to see you?" she asked.

"I don't know the whys of Michael's life. I know though that I have to be here. I know that I am here for other women going down the same path as I am."

"How can you do it?" she asked again.

"It's my one connection to Michael where I can see him," she said. "For a while that's all I could do. Then last year Angel's mother came in. He was involved in a holdup where the other guy killed someone too. Valoria, that's Angel's mother, was all upset. 'My baby's in prison with a murderer', she said. 'I am worried sick about him.'"

"I found out it was Michael," she smiled. "Angel was his cellmate. It was my connection. Valoria lives in San Luis, four hours away. She has a mother she has to take care of and younger kids. I told her that I would visit Angel. I do it, and that's how I find out about Michael."

"Every Sunday I bring Angel something that he can have—sometimes cookies, sometimes candy bars. I ask him to give some to

Michael, but I don't know if he does. He tells me what he can about Michael, but then sometimes nothing. Angel is a nice kid, but I don't know if I can believe him."

"Believe him?" she asked.

"He told me this week that Michael was starting to talk a little about me," she said. "He said that Michael loved me. I said how would I know? Angel told me to look for a sign and I said what sign? Angel said he didn't know."

She sipped coffee. "I have been waiting for a sign for three years and some days. I don't know whether he'll ever talk to me again or whether he's ok. I sometimes think it would have been easier if I had died as well. Sometimes I wished he was dead."

Brittany could not think of anything to say. For probably four minutes they sat in silence in Starbucks. With all her complaining about her dad, her brother and her mom, she knew that she was loved. Then something moved her to take the other chair and then she hugged the woman with the ponytail. Some singer started singing *I'll Be Home for Christmas* on the sound system.

They left without saying anything else. When Brittany got home, she made a call. "Mom," she said, "I think you'll be a great social worker."

"Really? What makes you say that?" The voice was surprised and pleased.

"Because you're a great listener."

"Thank you," she said. "I needed to hear that. How about coming for dinner sometime soon?"

"Sure. I'll come anytime this week. Can I see you on Christmas Eve?"

"Sure honey, but I thought you'd be with your dad."

"I will, but I want to see you both. Love you, Mom."

"Love you too."

Then she made another call. "Dad, I hope your trip to LA went well; call me when you can." She paused and added "I love you." She left the message.

The final call was to her brother. "Hey squirt," she said. "How about going skiing with me on Saturday?"

"You mean it?" he said, his voice squeaking high.

"Yeah, Dad's buying."

He laughed. "I love it when you laugh," Brittany said. "You sound so cool."

She never saw Donna again so she didn't know whether Donna ever got her sign, but she remembered that Monday as the day she had gotten her own.

Three Queens

The sky was full of stars that December 24th but not one seemed bright enough to lead him home.

Home was where his mother was probably putting the oysters into the milk. David's mother made oyster stew every Christmas, like her mother made, as part of their Christmas tradition. His stepfather had been home since four because the shop closed early that day, finishing his daily six pack by six. Another tradition. His little sisters were busy counting and sorting the presents under the tree; Etta making sure that Edie had no more, no less than she had. At seven and five, those numbers were very important.

David's numbers were important too. He was 103 miles away from home. He had been gone ninety-four days and had eight dollars left in his billfold. He had been stood almost fifty-eight minutes without a car passing by on the lonely Nebraska road. On this Christmas Eve, no one seemed to be travelling anywhere. With his luck, if anyone drove by, they'd still leave him standing by the edge of the road.

David wouldn't blame them; picking up a guy on a lonely road would feel dangerous, even on Christmas Eve. It was his own fault that he was out there. Why had he fallen asleep in the warm cab of the semi as soon as it left Colorado, thus missing his exit? Then why had he taken the ride with the young couple going further east than he wanted to go on his journey home? Was it bad luck that he had left his gloves in their car when he got out or was he just careless? The biggest why of all was why had he left his home in the first place?

Leaving seemed the right thing to do. David fought with Chad, his stepdad, all the time, leaving his mom caught in the middle. Mary had been with Chad eight years, but with her son for sixteen. His Grandpa and Grandma Stevens let the boy and his mother live with them on their farm which David loved. Then Grandma and Grandpa moved to town, leaving David and his mom on the farm alone. The year his grandparents died, Chad came along. In third grade Chad and his mother married, and then his little sisters were born. His happy life went further to hell with his stepfather losing job after job, and drinking and fighting with everyone who crossed his path. Etta and Edie were the only good things that came from those eight years.

High school was an even bigger hell than grade school. Chad kept saying David should get a job and pull his own weight, instead of thinking about scholarships and college. At school David was the skinny kid with tons of zits on his face who didn't play sports. His good grades didn't help anything. He was an alien from a foreign planet in a town where football ruled.

David knew he had made mistakes. He was suspended from school for three days when he had yelled at Rigley, the social studies teacher who happened to be the football coach as well. The jerk had said that nothing good came out of the first Gulf War. David's dad died in that war, and David wasn't going to let anyone badmouth the dad he had never known, even if his dad didn't know what they were fighting for.

Then Chad picked a fight with his mother about the suspension. "He's living a myth about his father," Chad said. "You've created this myth and there's no way I can meet it, even though I raised the damn kid, and he never knew his dad." Then he hit her.

"You shouldn't have made him mad," Mary told David after Chad went to the bar. So if he left, David figured maybe Chad couldn't get angry at David and his mother wouldn't get hit.

Taking his savings of $320, David had gone to Denver. Denver had been fine in October with seventy degree temperatures. He found a job working a parking lot for the Bronco games on the weekends, and then panhandled a little during the week. At night he slept in a park near the stadium. With his savings, he bought a sleeping bag and a backpack to store his few things.

On the first day of winter a front came through warm Denver and three older guys took his sleeping bag and pack. He let it all go so he didn't get beat up. Chad would have called him a wuss but David knew when the game was over. They took his money too and that was when he decided to head home. Even Chad was better than sleeping outside in the winter. He was beat.

David didn't want to go back completely empty-handed so after Denver's first snow of the season, he shoveled walks for people for two days. He bought a heavier coat at Goodwill and a cap like his Grandpa Stevens used to wear fishing, with funny furry ear flaps. That left $10 and he bought his mother's favorite, a box of chocolate covered cherries, and took off for home. He wanted to get his sisters something, but he worried he might need the money.

It had been easy catching the ride to Nebraska. The trucker and David had talked for a while but David was exhausted from the shoveling and trying to sleep outside. The cab of the big rig was warm, so warm that David fell asleep until he was 60 miles past his exit. The trucker felt bad so he bought David a cup of coffee and a burger at Wendy's. "Take care, buddy," the trucker had said. "Your folks are going to be glad to have you home."

David didn't know whether that was true or not; he just knew he wanted to be back at Logston. He had lost a lot of time. "You're so stupid," Chad's voice said in his head.

A young couple picked him up outside of the Wendy's. "We're going to Arnold," they said when he asked for a lift to Logston.

"Could you let me off at that turn-off for Valentine and I'll head up that way?"

"You sure you want to do it that way?" the 20-year-old guy said. "You might get a more direct shot to Valentine if you wait and you'll go through Logston."

"Or maybe call your mom," the girl said. "She'd come get you."

"No, tonight is the Christmas Eve service. I'll be there when they get home and surprise them." He also didn't want to take the chance that his mom wouldn't come and get him. That thought kept him awake and from missing the turn-off.

"Here," the girl said, handing him a thermos an hour later, "you can have our coffee." Then they left him off where the road divided with one route going to Arnold and the other to Valentine. As they drove off, David knew almost immediately that he had left his gloves in in the back seat. "You'd lose your head if wasn't fastened on," Chad's voice said. The road was snow-packed and slick in places so he stayed in one spot, watching the sun go down and a sliver of the moon rise. The wind was still, but the night felt raw. He was glad he had at least his Goodwill jacket and his hat on, but his fingers were cold even in the pockets. "Stupid kid," Chad said in his head. "You are not smart enough to go to college. Maybe you'll join the army like that father of yours."

At about six-thirty, he wished he had his sleeping bag more than a college scholarship. He thought about curling up in the ditch and just falling asleep. Then he drank all the coffee that was no longer hot and went from shivering to not shivering.

Finally a car came from the northeast, headed to North Platte. He didn't care anymore; he'd go back there and wait until morning.

It was a fancy pink car with large fins in the back, a huge boat of a car. Two women sat in front and a woman sat in the back with a black and white long-haired dog jumping all over, and barking like crazy—not growling or acting ferocious but greeting David like he was his long-lost friend. "Hello," the woman in the passenger front seat said through the open window. "Get in. You must be freezing."

He was too cold to talk as he crawled in. "You poor thing," the lady in the back crooned. "Bliss, stop licking him."

"It's alright," the boy could hardly talk, but even so he remembered how Charlie, his dog, had been when he was kid—so happy every day when he came home from school as if he had been gone a year. The black lab had been with him before Chad came, but when Chad moved in, Charlie had to go.

The collie wiggled back and forth, from David to the woman sitting in the back. The woman was middle-aged with curly black hair sticking out from under a white furry hat. Her coat was bright red matching her lipstick and her cheeks.

"Where are you going?" the driver said as she slowly pulled back out on the road going towards North Platte.

David still could hardly talk. "Logston…. before you get to Valentine."

"Ok, here we go." She swung the big car around on the snow packed road as if it was nothing. "We're going to California. We have had enough winter for a lifetime," she said.

Then she turned around and stared at David. Her long gray hair streamed like a lion's mane only tight with ringlets. Her skin was a light cocoa color but her eyes were deep midnight black. A pair of long, gold loop earrings and a gray cashmere sweater made her look like the women he had seen Christmas shopping at Macy's Department Store where he had shoveled for eight bucks an hour.

"You don't have to," David tried to tell her as she drove. Then the woman next to him took his rough hands. Hers were soft and warm.

"Hope, crank up that heater. His hands are like icicles. Baby, rub them together. Can you feel them?"

"Yes. You really don't have to turn around...."

The woman driving said nothing, but the car picked up speed.

They passed an orange diamond sign but all David saw was the word Detour. "Ma'am, I don't think you can go this way."

"What's your name, young man?" the driver asked in a voice like a high school principal.

"David...David Stevens."

"Well, Mr. David Stevens, we're taking you to Logston," the driver said in a loud, raspy voice. "We weren't going to California tonight anyway. California's not going anywhere, at least not tonight. It will probably fall into the ocean but it's ok for a few more years."

"Eve, don't talk that way. He's just a kid." The woman in the front passenger seat spoke gently. She turned and gave him a warm smile. She looked like the woman in front except that her hair was red and long. She wore a black fur hat, with a matching jacket like the woman sitting next to David. A single rhinestone earring dangled from her right ear.

"Hope, I am just telling him that we're going to take him home, and there's no and's, if's, or but's about it," Eve said. "Faith, you got any of those sandwiches left?"

"Sure do," the woman next to him spoke. David noticed another single rhinestone earring dangling from her right ear. "Bliss ate a couple of them, but there's two or three ham ones left. I forgot all about them. David, would you like to have them?"

"Thank you, but I had a burger in Lexington."

"Sweetie," the passenger in the front seat spoke, "it's no trouble. We only do what we want. Good grief, young man, where have you been?" she asked.

"Away. You really didn't need to turn around. I can wait in North Platte."

"Alright, who is driving this car?" the woman called Eve said, with a hoarse laugh. "I tell you if you hadn't been here giving us a diversion, I was going to go crazy. I was getting so sick of Hope and Faith that it's possible that they would have been stuck on the road in the middle of nowhere. Eat those sandwiches." She said it so strongly that he knew it would be foolish to disobey.

"Now, Eve, what do you mean by that?" Hope, the woman next to the driver, spoke up, her soft voice a little louder than before.

"You know what I mean, Hope," Eve said. "You two go bopping around life like nobody's business. 'Oh, it will work out just fine...' she said in a high pitched mimicking voice.

"Eve, I hate it when you talk like I talk that way," Faith said. "I just think Daddy was right when he'd say trust in me with all your heart."

"And besides," Hope said, "we always can hope for the best and that it will work out alright. You believe that, don't you....?" she said looking for his name.

"David. My name is David. I don't know." He hadn't had the best for a long time, and he didn't know how it would work out. Hope had left the farm when Chad moved in. "The best wasn't when some guys beat me up and took my stuff in Denver."

"Maybe not..." Faith said, touching his arm and then taking his hand. "Maybe though if that hadn't happened, you wouldn't be headed home to your mother. You know if we hadn't almost hit Bliss, she'd still be running loose off I-90. Now she's warm and safe, just like you."

David's hands still felt icy cold, but this was better than being outside. "You picked up a stray dog off the highway?" David asked. Then he wondered how she knew he was going to his mother. Guess that made sense; he looked like he was 14 and not 16.

"Yes, we did," Hope said, "and, like you, Bliss wasn't sure if that was such a hot idea either."

"But," Faith added, "I bet she knows it will turn out alright."

"She thinks she'll get another sandwich," Eve said. "That's what's making you her best friend right now."

"Do you think Daddy will like her?" Faith asked.

"Of course, he will," Eve said. "You two and Daddy are all alike.... he'd like that dog even if she had rabies."

"Are you sisters?" David asked.

"My goodness, yes. Hope and I are identical twins; Eve is our older sister."

"Do you always have to say older?" Eve said, turning to give Faith a dirty look. "I just happened to come along before you did."

"Oh, Eve, if you weren't older, you would still act as if you knew everything." Hope said it as if this was something that she had said many times before.

"Well, I know what I know because I have been connected with Daddy longer than you both."

"Longer—yes," Faith said, "but Hope and I both have our own special relationship with Daddy. Agreed?"

"Oh, of course," Eve said. "You both came along and had your own unique relationship with Daddy, just like everyone who has ever met him. I just happened to be the first. What's your family like, David?"

He groaned. "My mom is nice, but she married a... an idiot named Chad when I was eight. Then there are my sisters—Etta and Edie. They're cute, but they're just kids. I can't describe them more than that."

"Really?" Hope asked. "I always think kids are pretty established on who they are by then. Their personalities already shine."

"That's true," David said after a second or two. "Etta, the oldest, is like my mom. She can deal with little things going wrong and still keep going. Edie, on the other hand, gets frustrated if we're playing a game, and will walk off mad if she's not winning. I guess she's a little like Chad, but she's not mean like he is. She doesn't blame everybody else for what happened. Right now, they're probably both so excited about Christmas that they can hardly talk about anything else." The thought about his little sisters in pajamas on Christmas morning made him smile.

"What did you get them?" Hope asked.

His smile went away. "I didn't get them anything. I'm a little low on funds. I picked up a box of chocolate covered cherries for my mom, but nothing for the girls."

"Or your step-dad," Faith said.

"No. There's no way I'd get Chad anything even if I was rich," he said, crossing his arms.

"Those girls are just going to love having their big brother home," Faith said. "I just know it. And their mom too."

"Children are the greatest gifts," Eve said much more quietly than before. "You know, when a son dies….it just about kills a mother. And then to have your other son disappear. I know I am supposed to accept it, but to even think about it after all these years, it's very hard. …" her voice trailed off.

I must be dreaming. Eve sounded like his grandmother talking about his dad. *These women are too strange to be real.*

"What is real," Hope said, "is knowing that all things work out eventually." She touched her sister's cheek which shone even more with a few tears, and Hope then looked back at David. "Your mother will be happy beyond measure once she knows you're safe and home again. Chad will not be able to hurt you or your mother anymore because you're different than when you went to Denver. You'll face your problems head on."

"I hope so," David said. "I just don't know."

"Hope is where you start," his companion in the back seat said. "You can't have faith without hope....look at me. I had nothing when Abraham left me, nothing except my little boy. Now I am the largest Mary Kay dealer in the Midwest. And I tell you, Eve, if you would just use a little of that face cream like Hope and I do, you'd look younger too." The driver just shook her head as the car swerved on the snow packed road, but she didn't slow down any.

I must be dreaming...or maybe that coffee was spiked with something by those kids from Arnold.

"Honey," Hope said, "it starts out as a dream of what's needed or wanted or hoped for," and then her twin joined in.

"Then faith comes along and makes it happen. You don't know why three women in a pink Cadillac are out on the road in the middle of nowhere, but they are....and they're taking you home to Logston," Faith added.

"You're confusing the boy," Eve said, watching David through the rear view mirror. "Remember when you were little how your Grandma Stevens used to tell you Bible stories?"

He remembered. By now he was no longer shocked by what these women knew. Grandma Stevens would tell him stories before his mom came home from work, and his grandfather was finishing chores. "She'd be cooking something that smelled so wonderful and telling me about David fighting Goliath or the Israelites wandering for 40 years, but she didn't make it sound like the minister did," he said. "She made it feel real to me. I'd ask her if it was real...and she'd say, 'I don't know if it happened, but I know it's true.' I never understood that. It doesn't make sense, does it?"

"Does it matter if what happened really happened," Faith asked, "if we just need the message?"

"The truth," Eve said, "was that your father loved you, even if he never met you, because of the man he was. The truth is that your mother loves you and has done the best she knew how, even if she married Chad. The truth is that you're on your way home, and it will be alright."

All of a sudden, the pink Cadillac fishtailed and then slid to a halt, almost hitting the road barricade blocking the road. There was no bridge over Old Widow Creek. "I guess here's the reason no one was headed to Logston," Eve said.

All four scrambled out of the car and looked at the twenty foot gap in the road. On both sides, the embankment was steep and full of snow. Bliss immediately did her business next to the car and then started romping around the car.

"Daddy always said humans should be as happy as dogs," Hope said watching Bliss frolic.

"I don't see what there is to be happy about," David said. "This feels just as bad as when I was standing on the road an hour ago. My hands are cold again, and it's too far to walk without freezing tonight. If we go back the other way, I won't make it home for Christmas Eve. I feel as bad as if I was still in Denver, maybe even worse since I am this close and yet so far."

"I know," Eve said. "It seems as far as away as it did when you were in Denver. But it will be alright." She stood in the snow with tall black boots and her flowing sweater wrapped around her, towering over David and her sisters.

"It will be alright David," Hope said putting her arms around his shoulders, giving him a hug.

"David," Faith said, "you'll get home tonight." Turning to Eve she said, "Give me the keys. Now!"

Without a word of discussion, Eve tossed her the keys. Then Hope and Eve crawled into the back seat. Eve whistled for Bliss who bounded into the back seat and shook herself of snow, sprinkling the woman with white crystals. Still without a word, Faith motioned to David to get in the front and then both crawled in. She backed up the Caddy almost half a mile. "I hate it when she drives," Hope said as Bliss whined softly.

"I heard that," Faith said and then gunned it. David looked at the speedometer...80, 90...112 miles per hour on the snow packed road. The car crashed through the barrier and sailed over the creek.

She skidded to a stop after they landed, making a full 360 degree turn. "What do you think now, Mr. Stevens?" Faith sounded just like Eve and the two in the back joined in laughing while David caught his breath.

"Oh, let's sing Christmas carols on the way in," Hope said as Faith started driving the car again. "Dashing through the snow..."

They all joined in singing songs that Grandma Stevens had taught him as a little boy.

"Let's teach David the one I wrote," Eve said and in her raspy voice, she started.

"We, Three Queens of Nebraska, are
Traveling in a Cadillac car
Through the ice and through the snow
Following yonder star
Oh...Oh....
Star of Wonder, Star of Light
Star with radiant beauty bright
Westward leading, still proceeding
Guide us to the perfect site...."

"Eve, honey, I don't think that as good as the original, "Hope said. "You're missing the point. For one thing, we're not going west anymore."

"Well, keep heading east and eventually you wind up west! Just be quiet, and let me sing," Eve insisted. She continued:

David, we found cold by the road
His heart was carrying too heavy a load
Lost and tired, scared and worried
So far away from home...
Oh...Oh....
Star of Wonder, Star of Light
Star with radiant beauty bright.
Westward leading, still proceeding
Guide us to the perfect site....

Mary, his mother, waits on the farm
Her son to come and hold in her arms
She cooks, she cleans, she hopes, she prays.
That he's safe from harm.
Oh...Oh....
Star of Wonder, Star of Light
Star with radiant beauty bright
Westward leading, still proceeding
Guide us to the perfect site....

"And another thing your rhyme isn't tight," Faith said.

"I like it," David said. "It reminds me of my grandpa." Eve reached up front and gave a nudge on the shoulder like his grandpa used to. Then for the first time in eight years, David sang the version of *Three Kings* that his grandpa did..."We, three kings of orient, are..."

"Smoking on a rubber cigar…" the three sisters joined in together singing.

"Look. There are the lights of Logston," Faith said, interrupting the singing. "You want to go to the farm, right, David?"

Without waiting for his answer, she drove west through town, by the cemetery and out the oil road. By the time they were making the corner mile, he could see the barn light on the white barn, shining bright, across the field.

"I see it!" he said. "I see it!" The place of his childhood had never looked more beautiful.

They crossed the little creek before the driveway, but before turning in, Faith stopped the car.

"This is it," she said. "You get to walk the driveway."

He was confused. The driveway had six inches of snow on it, but they had plowed through more. He got out anyway and so did the sisters. Bliss danced around the women and David.

"Take Bliss," Hope said. "She can be the girls' present."

"They'd like that a lot," he said. "Thank you so much." He hugged Hope hard. The other two sisters wrapped their arms around him, and David finally felt warm all over, even his hands.

"You'll be ok," Faith said.

"They'll be so happy that you're home," Eve said, a little tearfully.

"You won't be alone ever again," Hope said. "Take these gloves." Reaching into her pocket she pulled out bulky gloves like his grandfather had worn.

Bliss started running down the driveway. "I better go," he said. "Merry Christmas!"

He started down the driveway and then looked back after a few seconds. The car was gone. Except for his footprints behind him and the dog tracks ahead, the snow lay perfect, undisturbed. He didn't care what had happened; he was home. With a burst of energy, he started running down the driveway, with Bliss leading the way.

When he opened the kitchen door, Bliss ran in ahead, like she had been there a thousand times before. His mother was stirring something on the stove and Etta was setting the table. She dropped a plate when she saw him and the dog, but it didn't break.

"David," his mother gasped. Then his mother, Etta, and Edie were hugging him, and he felt the same way he did at the end of the driveway, warm all over. Bliss was jumping and licking the girls.

"You came home for Christmas," Mary said, after two minutes of tight hugging. She was crying, just like Eve had been.

"And a dog…you brought us a dog!" Edie said with tears of joy in her eyes. Bliss was wagging all over. His sisters immediately dropped to their knees, cooing over the collie and wiping the snow off.

"I did. Do you like her?" he asked.

Etta looked up. "It's almost as good as you being here."

"Where's Chad?" he asked after a moment.

His mother smiled. "He doesn't live here anymore." The little girls petted the dog who wagged her tail as if she was beating a drum.

"David, how did you get here?" Edie asked.

"Well, I'll tell you the story," David said. "I don't know if it happened, but I know it's true. But could we have some oyster stew first?"

Friends of Animals, Suckers, and Lost Souls Center

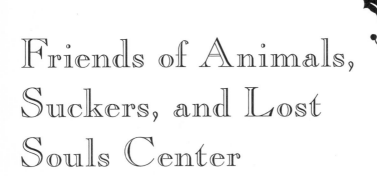

"Hey, you know what my dad did as a kid?" a voice came out of nowhere in the dark. "He and my uncle set a cat on fire and then their fucking house caught on fire." Laughter filled the cold night air.

Walking from the Salvation Army Thanksgiving dinner, Joe heard the voices in the alley by the Alright Parking Lot. He ducked behind a big van until he knew for sure what was happening.

Joe had been hoping he would find someone who had something to top off his full stomach. It would be sweet if somebody had some grass, but the crowd at the Thanksgiving dinner didn't include stoners, but instead old men and women missing teeth, or else tired moms with lots of kids, or Spanish speaking families with even more tons of kids and a tiny abuela to boot. He'd be lucky if he'd get enough beer for a buzz, let alone grass.

There were more voices and laughter, and then a voice said, "Let's see if she'll light." Then a god awful yowl and a small ball of fire ran past him where he hid behind the van. *Son of a bitch. They lit a cat on fire.*

The taste of pumpkin pie came back up his throat. *Don't let them see me.* Then he thought of Mikey.

Mikey was the closest person he had to a friend the last three years. The kid was a lot younger than Joe and even more messed up after two years in Iraq. Mikey's folks tried to help him, but he left them back in the Midwest and lived on the streets along Cherry Creek in downtown Denver. Joe bonded with the kid and they slept together a lot in the alley or under bridges. It was good to have a buddy to keep you safe and ward off the jackals. He got Mikey's jacket and pack after the kid ran into the street when he thought some screaming music was a jihadist attack. "Don't let them see me," he said right before he died in Joe's arms. The guys in the SUV just kept driving.

He thought he had hit rock bottom then. Nothing mattered. Five years ago his sister hunted him down for his mom's funeral, but what was the point? He hadn't seen her alive in the last four years when he lived on the street so why bother now when she was dead?

"Debra will be there," Karla, his sister, said.

"So?" he said. "I don't have anything to say to her." The last years of their marriage had dried up whatever there was to say.

"She'd at least tell you how Tawnie's doing."

"And then she'll tell Tawnie what a loser or a son of bitch she has for a father. What's the point?"

"You are a son of a bitch," Karla said. "You don't give a damn about anything. You never have."

That wasn't true. He really liked Mikey. Mikey was a little older than Tawnie, but he could have been Joe's son. Protecting Mikey made him feel useful. He held the kid when Mikey had the flashbacks and kept him safe. If Joe hadn't been drunk that night, the kid would still be here. If he hadn't been drunk at work, he wouldn't have lost the job and then the house and maybe he'd still be with Debra and Tawnie.

Mikey had made him a better person which had taken a lot of effort. Joe had kind of redeemed himself, as much as he could be redeemed, after fucking it up with Debra and Tawnie. But now he was gone. The noise of the punks brought him back to reality in downtown Denver. *God, I should have stayed at the mission.* It was too cold to sleep out and now he'd have a hard time getting a bed. Of course, if these punks beat him up, he'd end up at Denver General Hospital.

Hey, that wouldn't be too bad. He'd have a bed, and warmth, and something to eat, if they left him any teeth.

Last time he'd run afoul of guys almost mean enough to set a cat on fire, he had gone to a dentist who the shelter said would look him over. "You need a bridge," a dentist named Lieberman told him. "I can't fix it otherwise."

"I don't have the money," Joe told him.

"Gee, you got money for beer somehow," Lieberman said, like he was cleaning pigeon shit from his car. "Did you cut your cheek to get that lovely swastika? No money for a tattoo?"

Joe left the office without saying anything and spent the last of his beer money on something a kid said was Percocet. He had liked Percocet when his back hurt from his construction job. It relieved the pain in his mouth but hadn't helped the pain from his embarrassment. Joe had handled losing his wife, daughter, and house without being embarrassed. He took the money that his sister rationed off every month that his mother left him without feeling too bad because he drank half a bottle of vodka after he saw Karla each time. After this long on the street, Joe didn't embarrass easily, but he was still embarrassed about that mark on his cheek.

He'd been hanging out with a bunch of skinheads, mostly because they were smoking and drinking and giving him stuff to smoke. "You Jewish?" one had said to him out of the blue.

"No, I am not Jewish," he said. "Why would you say that?"

"You said your name was Schneider. That sounds Jewish."

"Schneider's German. I grew up Catholic." As soon as he said it, he knew that was as equally a stupid and risky thing to say. "But I hate Catholics," he said hoping they would let it go. "Bunch of the top guys wearing dresses, like fags."

Then another guy looked coldly at him. "I am Catholic." There was a dead silence and then the five guys started laughing.

"And I hate you…." another said, hitting his friend in the shoulder. "But not as much as niggers or Jews."

Joe was so buzzed he wanted to smack someone, one of these white jerks. "Yeah, Jews are the worst. I hate them," he said instead.

"Hey, I got an idea," the guy who said it started laughing. "Let's give Joe an early Christmas gift."

"I don't need anything," he said, immediately feeling nervous.

"Yeah you do. I am going to give you a tattoo…. a homemade kind."

The Catholic skinhead took a knife out of his pocket and two other guys held him down. Then with six sharp moves or so, his cheek was cut. The blood dripped down onto his lips.

"Son of a bitch!" Joe yelled. "What the fuck are you doing?"

"Now any Jewish asshole that you hate will know enough to stay away from you."

"Yeah, but that hurts." He tried now to make light of it because he knew sometimes guys like this enjoyed seeing you squirm, the more, the better. He didn't want to motivate the idiot into hurting him even more.

"Get over it. I don't want to waste money on a real tattoo on a drunk like you."

Joe said nothing more. The guy who cut him laughed once more, got up, and walked away.

One by one they followed until the last one stopped and bent over him, and said, "Here, get some antiseptic." He dropped a ten dollar bill on him.

Joe's fingers were bloody after he touched his face. He shook when he stood up, felt the blood again and then touched the ten dollar bill. He went over to the 7-11 and used the bathroom.

There was a swastika on his face after he cleaned off the blood. He bought beer instead of antiseptic. The clerk looked at him oddly but said nothing.

Now two years later he tried to avoid looking at his face as much as possible. Sometimes when his face was dirty, you couldn't see the mark, but when it was clean, it was clear. Sometimes he thought about cutting himself again, to make it just an ugly scar instead of the ugliest symbol in the world. He had enough pain without seeking out more. With his luck, he'd wind up cutting a hole straight through his face and all the beer would leak out of his cheek.

"I don't even know any Jews," he said to himself every time he washed his face. "Just other assholes."

Black kids beat him up the next time, knocking out some of his teeth. He couldn't win for losing with the blacks or the whites. Or Jewish dentists.

The voices faded down the street finally. He walked over to the dumpster and a pile of boxes where the jerks had found the cat. He didn't want to see it, but he kind of wondered if it was dead. Maybe if he saw it, he'd kill it just to put it out of his misery. Bunch of dopes.

Maybe they had dropped some dope. He didn't know who these kids were, but kids out this late were as dangerous as black dudes or white supremacists when it came to people like him.

He was digging through the trash when one of the boxes moved.

"Shit," he said pulling back. Under the box was a kitten so small it fit into his hand. "Was that your mama?" he asked the gray kitten whose eyes weren't even opened. Then he remembered. The mama was on fire.

It made some kind of squeaky noise, not a meow, but a squeak. It looked like a hairless mouse, and he remembered the summer he spent on Uncle Eddie's farm. There were five kittens in the barn. He and Karla loved petting them and giving them milk. Then one morning they came out to find all the kittens dead.

"King Herod came through," his uncle said when he found them crying.

"King Herod?" Joe said confused.

"Yeah, tomcats sometimes come through and kill all the kittens. Don't know why, but they do. They're sons of bitches," he said, throwing the dead kittens into the manure pile.

"Sons of bitches," Joe said out loud to the kitten. "That's who killed your mama." The kitten shivered in his palm.

Shit. Thanksgiving night with a little kitten. Nobody at the shelter would take him in or help with it; they were too overwhelmed with just the guys from the street. Then he remembered a vet place he used to go by on Federal Boulevard. Its sign said Open, 7 Days a Week, 24 Hours a Day. Friends of Animals Veterinary Center.

Thanksgiving night had to be right up there with the worst night of the year to work. Rachel Lebowitz's vet on call had cancelled so she was at the clinic herself. Already she had operated on a dumb Labradoodle who had eaten the whole turkey carcass that a college boy had left on the counter. If the dog hadn't perforated his stomach, she would have left it alone after she did surgery, but now she felt uneasy about leaving the dog and going to sleep in her comfortable bed.

Rachel had sat with her dad many a night at the Friends of Animals Veterinary Center after her mother had died when she was eleven. He took in strays, canines, felines, birds and a few humans. She had lost her faith in humanity after being broken into one too many times and started carrying a gun to keep the fear and men at bay. Animals were much safer, and she knew where she stood with them. She was their doctor, not their friend, but she did everything she could to keep them healthy.

Until nine that night it had been quiet. She had been looking at the Facebook page Jesse, her receptionist, had created for her: Doc R at the Friends of Animals Center. She had 1,245 friends already, thanks to Jesse, but she knew none of them. But that was how Bailey, the Labradoodle, had come in, thanks to a friend of a friend she didn't know.

The drunk college guy wept on her couch when she said the dog might die. "It's my girlfriend's dog," he said. "You can't let it die."

"I am not Jesus," she said, always enjoying the irony of a Jew saying that. "But I'll do what I can."

"Thank you so much." The kid sounded as if he would cry again. Rachel was too tired to care. *Keep an eye on your girlfriend's dog if you love her so much.*

"Yeah, come by tomorrow and we'll see what's next."

She lay on the office couch, curled up in a quilt that she kept there for nights like this, half listening for the sound of the dog in distress. Instead she heard a bang, bang, bang on the door at about 11:30.

"What do you want?" she shouted as she pulled out the Ruger that she kept in the desk drawer and then stuck it into her jeans, and slipped on her lab coat loosely.

"I've got a kitten," a shaky voice said.

She moved closer so she could see out the one way window. A guy in an army jacket hunched over something. "Let me see it," she said sounding as tough as she could. "Frank, can you come here?" she called to an imaginary helper.

The guy held out his two hands. A gray kitten, maybe not a day old, she guessed.

She opened the door. "Where did you get that kitten?"

The guy's nose was running and he wiped it on his shoulder. "I found it."

"Where its mother?" she asked wondering why a sick Labradoodle and a newborn orphan kitten were happening to her this evening. *Why is God mad at me?*

"I think she's dead," the voice said sadly and when she took the kitten from him, he told about the kids who set the cat on fire.

"Did you get a look at them?" *I'd set them on fire myself if I was close enough to look at them.*

"No, I didn't want them to think it would be fun to set me on fire."

She looked at him, a street guy like lots downtown. He didn't scare her, not as long as she had the gun close.

"This kitten needs a mother," she said looking at the kitten. "Or at least some warmth. And something to drink. Stay here."

She went back and briefly looked at Labradoodle exhausted after his deadly feast, curled up in a ball. *At least someone's sleeping.*

"Wrap this baby up, she said, handing the guy a piece of flannel the size of a washcloth, when she came back. "Hold it next to your chest." The kitten kept squeaking.

"Maybe it's hungry," the man offered.

"Maybe, but we have to warm it up first. You look like you need warming up too. You want some coffee?" It was the gentlest her voice had been.

"Yeah, that would be good."

She came back with two cups steaming. "Thanks," the guy said. She looked at him closer. Like a lot of street guys, he looked like he could be thirty or fifty years old. Dirty jacket, stocking cap on his head, interesting cheek. "Where did you find the cat?" she asked, deciding to ignore further examining him.

"Down by the Civic Center."

"That's a good distance. Why did you bring him here?" she asked. "How did you know that I'd be here?"

"I used to work over at the Federal Center. I transferred in front of your clinic. I took a chance you'd still be here."

"Lucky for the kitten." She gave it a small smile.

"Is it a boy?"

A loud retching noise came from the room behind her, preventing her from answering.

"Damn it," she said and rushed into the next room. The dog rolled in blood with more coming from its mouth and rear end every second.

"What's happening?" the guy asked.

"I don't know," she said. "Maybe I missed a bone or else the intestines are twisted. Put that kitten in your pocket. You're going to help me."

"What?" he said

"Just shut up and do what I tell you!" All gentleness was gone.

He stared at her, put the kitten in the pocket of his jacket, and nodded grimly.

She drew something into a syringe and then lifted the dog up onto the counter. She gave it a shot and the poor dog stopped moving almost immediately. Quickly, she put on some gloves, and before he could look away, she put a tube down the dog's throat and turned on a machine. Then she took a scalpel, and made a cut on the dog's already bare stomach. "Wash your hands," she said, "and put gloves on," nodding at a box on the counter.

The guy looked sick at the sight of all the blood, but he did as she told him. "Ok, what you're doing is holding this apart while I look for bones that I might have to pick out." She gestured at the cut with her nose.

She worked quickly "Nope, it's the gut. There's the twist." She pulled out about eight inches of red angry gut and untangled it. Don't let it move," again nodding at the open spot as she carefully laid it back.

All of a sudden she was a mad woman. "Come on!" she ordered. "Come on! Don't stop now!"

"Squeeze that bag, 1001, 1002, 1003, squeeze," she nodded at the balloon bag hanging below the table. He held the bag that he hadn't even notice while she pressed on the chest of the dog. She breathed heavily, willing the muscle to move. "Squeeze, 1001, 1002, 1003," Then she took a deeper breath of relief. "Ok…it's going again."

"What happened?"

"The dog's heart stopped beating. We just did CPR on him." She had blood on her lab coat. "Sorry, I got you bloody too. Let me finish this up."

In a minute or two she had the dog sewed up. "Thank you," she said and then yawned as if she cut open a dog every day.

"What about the cat?" he said.

"It's probably going to die, but there are lot of cats in the world." Rachel shrugged.

"You'd save that dog," he said.

"Sure. The kid that owns it will pay me. You won't."

"Why not?" He seemed to ignore the bit about being paid.

"I am tired and I don't want to get up every four hours to feed a damn cat."

"I'll do it," he said, "but feed it what? Milk?"

"Not cow milk," she said. "We'll start out with some Pedialyte."

"Like for kids?" he asked.

"Yeah," she said, somewhat surprised. "You know what that is?"

"It's special water," he said. "We gave it to my daughter when she was little with an upset stomach."

"Works the same with kittens. With this guy, I don't know whether it's sick or cold or hungry or all three so we start slow. There weren't any other kittens, were there?"

He shook his head. "Did you look?" she said, looking at him critically.

"I didn't see anything, but it was cold, and I didn't want to be around in case those guys came back."

"You should have looked."

"Why? Aren't there plenty of cats around?" He looked mad, and she was glad she had remembered her gun.

"Ok but you're the one who will have to take care of it." She shrugged.

"I don't have any place to take care of a cat," he said. "I won't be able to take it into the shelter, and besides they won't let me in at this hour."

"You can sleep out in the entry way," she said. "It's warm enough. I've got the couch. If something happens, wake me up. We'll give it the Pedialyte, and then in four hours you'll do it again."

"How will I get it?"

I'll give it to you, but I am going to sleep in between. Then tomorrow we'll see how it's going. Ok?" She looked tired but still firm.

"Ok," he said. "I've slept in worse places."

"You got a sleeping bag or anything?" she asked.

"No, I don't, but I'll be ok." He sat down on the corner, looking out at Federal Boulevard and the cars going by.

"I'll get the Pedialyte." She left and came back with a little bottle with a nipple, plus another old blanket and a towel.

"Ok, cats don't necessarily know how to nurse so this is how you do it." She laid the towel down across his lap. "Put the kitty belly down. Now move the head to the nipple, slowly. Try to center it over the tongue. Good....just squirt a little bit." Almost immediately the kitten moved its head to the bottle. "Good kitty," she said. "You've got a smart one. Give it a little more."

"But this is just water."

"It will do," she said. "It doesn't need more. Tomorrow we'll give it some formula. Right now I am going to bed. I'll give you some more water at six."

"What time is it now?" Joe asked.

"Almost two," she answered. "Good night."

"Yeah, good night. Thank you, doc." He pulled his jacket collar up his neck.

Damn it, Rachel, do you have to adopt every stray that comes along? She lay down on the couch and fingered her gun.

He stroked the little kitten in his hand and then wrapped it up in the flannel before sticking it under his thermal underwear shirt that he wore under his sweatshirt. He was afraid if he kept his jacket closed, he might smother it.

Tawnie had been campaigning for a cat when he left the last time. "I'll take care of it," his daughter pleaded to Debra, who at that point thought with a ten-year-old daughter and a no-good husband she did not need another thing to take care of.

"No, I am not going to have another expense," she said. "We're barely making it on my two jobs."

"A cat doesn't take much," Joe had offered in support.

"No, but you do."

She was right. The part that had probably done the marriage in was that there was nothing specific that he or Debra could point to that had made him drink so much. At one time he had a good construction job; his family loved him; and things were going great. Then one by one, things crumbled, and he lost it all.

"You're just like Dad," Karla had said when she took him in the first month Debra told him to leave. "Only I am not Mom and Debra isn't Mom either. I'm not going to put up with this crap like she did."

And Karla didn't. He was gone by Christmas. He saw Tawnie once after that, at her high school graduation, but he hadn't talked to her. Just sat and watched her cross the stage with hundreds of other people. The more years went by, the more impossible it seemed to get together with his daughter. He still saw Karla every month to get his check from his mom's estate.

"Wake up." Doctor Rachel Lebowitz nudged him with her shoe. He hadn't realized he had been sleeping. She held a cup of coffee in her hand. She was wearing the blood stained coat but this time he saw her name tag. "It's time for the next feeding."

He pulled the little bundle out of his shirt. It squirmed a bit and made little noises.

"Ok, we're trying some fake milk now. But it's the same process."

She took the kitten from him. "You sleep it off?" she asked, eyes narrowing.

"I wasn't drunk," he said.

"Oh, really?" Rachel said. "You looked drunk to me."

Looking closer at her, he realized that she was probably Karla's age, mid 40s. Last night he thought she was young, but maybe that was because she was so small.

"What happened to the guy who owned this place?" he asked, ignoring her comment.

"He died," Rachel said.

"Every year, on the day before Christmas, he'd put out coffee for the people waiting for the bus."

She smiled her rare smile. She had forgotten that. Her dad had died in December and she had come home to make all the arrangements. There was no coffee that year. She hadn't celebrated Hanukah that year either. It was the last straw—her dad dying then. The next week she was broken into and some guys followed her one night. She came back to work with a gun, packed the Menorah away and just got the clinic up and running the day after Christmas. Boxing Day. She had unpacked her boxes and took care of dogs that had gotten into the chocolate covered cherries idiots had left under the tree.

"So you took over his business?"

"Yeah, I get along better with animals than I do people so it seemed like a good way to go."

"He'd give us coffee, and say, 'If you need me tomorrow, I am open,'" Joe smiled as he said it.

"We didn't celebrate Christmas," Rachel said.

At that he suddenly became aware of his scar. "I don't believe this crap," he said fingering the mark that felt like it must cover his entire face.

"I don't either," she said, "at least not the way the Germans used it. Did you know that before the Nazi assholes got hold of it, it was a symbol for goodness? It comes from India, and it literally means to be good."

He felt it again. *To be good*. That was so far away from how he usually felt. Usually feeling good meant feeling numb.

"Ok, baby's gotten enough. Now we need to get something out of him." The vet brought him back to the present.

"What do you mean?" he said.

"The kitten doesn't know how to shit or pee. We're going to help him. I would have done it last night, but I was kind of preoccupied with Bailey."

She gave him the kitten and a towel. "Rub him with this," handing him a washcloth. He gently rubbed the kitten. Then she gave him a handful of tissue. "Ok, rub his behind."

Joe wrinkled his nose a bit but he did.

"Shit," he said after a moment, looking at the excrement now on the tissue.

"Didn't know you went to vet school."

He laughed.

"So why are you on the street?" She sat down beside him.

He shook his head. He had no answer he could give to this woman, or Karla, or the social worker at the Rescue mission, or even Mikey. He got too shaky on the beams so he drank more. He couldn't handle the look his wife gave him when he drank so he drank more. He couldn't handle anything unless he drank more.

Yet it was almost ten hours since he had a drink. He had gone to sleep without having a drink within the last three hours. His hands were starting to shake when he remembered that he hadn't a drink. He sipped the coffee slowly.

"How's the dog?" he asked.

"So far, so good. I think we're out of the woods." She sighed.

"What's the matter?" he asked.

"I am just tired. I got to work at eight yesterday morning. I have been here all day and now night. It's six in the morning and I've had only a few hours of sleep." She yawned. "What's your name anyway?"

"Joe…. Joseph Schneider. Thanks for taking care of the kitten." He handed her the kitten. "I think I'll be going now."

"Wait a minute….are you just leaving the cat with me?" she said with exasperation.

"I am not able to take care of it."

"Well, I have got enough to do. If you want that cat to survive, you're going to be the one to make it happen. Otherwise, I'll give it a shot, and it will go to sleep."

"Don't you have to take care of animals? You're a veterinarian."

"Don't you have to be there for your daughter?" she asked. "Isn't that what fathers do?"

They stared at each other. "Why do you care?" he asked.

"I lost my dad when I was twenty-five. I know what it's like. I miss him every day. You're more worried about this little one-day-old cat than a human being."

"What about you? Didn't you say you liked animals better than humans?"

"Maybe, but I didn't say I liked that I liked that."

He turned to leave. She stood up. "I swear. I'll put this kitten to sleep if you go out that door. I don't need one more thing to do today."

He stopped. "Alright, but I want more coffee."

She put him to work that morning cleaning out the cages. The animals didn't seem to care that they had not seen him before. By nine o'clock, however, Joe wasn't anywhere to be seen but Rachel didn't have time to deal with another lost sheep.

"Hey," Jesse, the tattooed receptionist, said when she came in five after nine. "There's a guy smoking in the back."

"Army jacket?"

"I don't know. It's green." Jesse was nineteen and worked cheap. That made up for her not knowing much.

Rachel went to the back. "What are you doing?" she yelled at Joe. He was standing, propped up against the dumpster, cigarette in his hand.

"I don't feel good," he said. "I think I am sick."

"You're probably going through withdrawal," Rachel looked at him. "When's the last time you had a drink?"

"I don't know....right before I ate the Thanksgiving dinner."

"How do you feel?" she asked.

"I've got a bad headache, and my hand won't stop shaking."

"I am sorry, but I can't help you. Go see Jesse, get some ibuprofen, and then get back to those cages."

"I don't think I can."

"Well, you better. Otherwise I am throwing your sorry ass out of here and the kitten right behind it."

At ten she came back to the front desk again. "Where's Joe?" she asked Jesse who was checking Facebook.

"The street guy? He's feeding the kitten," Jesse said. "How come he's here?"

"Showed up last night. Helped with the dog that ate the turkey."

"He's going to be worse before he's better," Jesse said. "I've seen my step-dad give up drinking gazillions of times. So why'd you get involved?"

"He came in with a kitten, a newborn kitten. You know I am a sucker for cats."

"You're really a sucker for people."

"Am not." Rachel stuck her chin out.

"Are too...otherwise how come I am here?" And the skinny girl smirked.

"You're here because you came in with an iguana....my first and only iguana patient. And you work cheap. How's Oscar doing anyway?"

"About the same. He's fine as long as a pit bull doesn't try to fight him. But don't change the subject."

"Yeah well, I am going back to work. And stay off Facebook. There's work to be done."

The day dragged on. At noon they put the "Back by 1" sign on the door, and Jesse heated up the turkey she brought in from Thanksgiving. "Want something to eat?" she said to Joe who was feeding the kitten again.

"I don't know if I can keep it down," he said. He looked like hell.

"How much do you drink?" Jesse asked.

He shrugged. "You're going through withdrawal," she said. "It's not going to be easy. How much do you drink a day?"

"Maybe a quart or two of beer, if I can get it. Sometimes some vodka."

Jesse looked at Rachel. "I brought something in for decoration," Jesse said, changing the subject.

"Not another Christmas tree, I hope," Rachel said. "Mrs. Singer's dog peed on it the first day last year, and then we had that ferret that climbed it and knocked it over, fizzling all the lights."

"No, this is simpler. It's an Advent wreath." Pulling out an artificial green wreath with five electric candles sticking in it, Jesse smiled and put it on the counter.

"Great. You're asking a Jewish vet to put out an Advent wreath."

"You always say you're an atheist."

"I am. God left the building about the time Elvis did." Rachel then giggled, more tired than amused.

"Huh?"

You're so young," Rachel said. "Besides, a Jew is always a Jew, whatever she believes."

"Is it Advent already?" Joe said, looking in from the fog that surrounded him.

"This Sunday marks the first week. The Candle of Hope," Jesse said. "Hey, can we get the Menorah out too? I saw it this summer when I was cleaning in the supply room."

"Have your candle of hope. But I don't see any reason to celebrate a myth about the miracle in the temple. There are no miracles, even though people hope for it."

"Hope was my mom's name," Joe said quietly.

The two women said nothing for a minute. "It's a good name," Jesse said finally.

"Maybe we could call the kitten that," Joe said.

He stood up, wavered and then toppled over and went into a seizure.

"Jesus," Rachel said, the second time in twenty-four hours. "Call 911."

The ambulance arrived in five minutes, the longest five minutes Rachel ever felt as Joe seized twice more. Rachel hadn't been this scared since the hospital called to tell her that her father was dead. Jesse held him down and Rachel helped and then he lay there in a pool of urine.

Rachel put the kitten in her pocket once she found where he had dropped it.

"He quit drinking recently," she told the EMTs.

"They go into seizures sometimes if it's bad enough. That's probably it. Any family?" the EMT asked. Then Joe started yelling. "I can't go. You'll kill Hope. Don't kill her, Debra. Please don't." His shouts were mixed with sobbing.

"Who's Debra?" the EMT asked.

Rachel whispered, "I have no idea. I just met him last night."

"Joe, listen to me. The kitten is going to be fine. You'll come back and see it. I will keep it for you." Jesse's voice was soothing even to Rachel.

"What will you do?" Rachel asked the attendant.

"We'll take him to Denver General, and then he'll probably end up in Detox there. You can get a restraining order if you want. He's a piece of work."

"He's not. He's good," Rachel said surprised at her words.

"Got a next of kin?"

"I am," Jesse spoke up. "Jesse Trebon. He's my uncle."

"When's his birthday?" the attendant asked, writing it down.

"Got me….we didn't celebrate together."

The attendant shook his head. "Whatever."

"I'll come down after work and see you Uncle Joe," Jesse said, committing to the role. "Don't worry about Hope."

"I think we're done for the day," Rachel huffed as the ambulance finally pulled away. "I need some sleep."

"Go to sleep. It will be better. I'll take care of the kitten," Jesse said.

"What a mess! And where the hell is that Labradoodle's owner? They were supposed to pick up Bailey. Why do people do this to me?"

"They don't do it to you. Stuff just happens," Jesse said. "I am going to light the candle."

"Whatever," Rachel said. "But give me the kitten."

Traffic was heavy as she drove with the shoppers coming back from their Black Friday shopping. Rachel curled up in an afghan on her couch at home but sleep didn't come so after two hours she put blue jeans back on and a hoodie, and drove downtown. She carried the kitten in an old stocking cap that had been her dad's, but left it in the car when she got to the hospital.

"Hi," she said to the woman at the front desk at Denver General. "I am Jesse Trebon. My uncle, Joseph Schneider, is here."

Without a smile or greeting, the woman typed something in the computer. "Yes, he's on the detox floor. That's the fourth floor." Then she went back to typing.

The tired woman walked over to the elevator. "Rachel," a voice called. "What are you doing?"

A good question indeed. She looked at Jesse. "I am a sucker for drunks, evidently, as well as iguanas, slacker college kids, cats and Labradoodles."

"I can get in because I am his next of kin," Jesse said, oddly proud. "I guess you're my moral support."

They rode the elevator and then walked down the hall to detox without saying anything. A security guard stood there. "Ladies, can I help you?"

"We're here to see my uncle, Joseph Schneider." Jesse sounded worried.

"And you are?" He asked looking at a clipboard.

"Jesse Trebon."

"And you?" He stared at Rachel.

"Dr. Rachel Lebowitz."

"You're a doctor? Making house calls?"

"Yes," she said with confidence. "I am Mr. Schneider's doctor and I am an advisor to Ms. Trebon."

"Whatever," the guard said and he opened up a door. "Joe, your niece is here. And your doctor."

He looked at them blankly, wrapped up in a blanket and dressed in a hospital gown. Then a smile came across his face. "Hello," he said.

"Uncle Joe," Jesse hugged him. Then he looked embarrassed in his hospital gown, and pulled it back together in the back. "How are you feeling?"

"Better," he said. "I had some really bad hallucinations for a while. I saw my friend Mikey, and then my daughter Tawnie, but I couldn't reach her. She was floating away." For a moment he looked as if he still was reaching. "So how is Hope?" he asked looking at Rachel.

"Doing well," Jesse said quickly. "Quite the miracle."

"Good. And Bailey?"

"Bailey's fine," Rachel said carefully, "but his owner's a jerk."

"Thank you for taking care of Hope," he said to Jesse, and then he laid down, closing his eyes.

"You're welcome. Is there anything you need us to do?"

He sighed. "Not today. But would you come back tomorrow?"

"After work," Jesse said. "We'll come together."

They didn't talk until they reached the elevator. "This is so going on Facebook," Jesse said, clicking a selfie on her phone "My mom is going to freak out when she hears I was in Detox."

On Saturday morning Bailey's owner came in with the guilty boyfriend. She had tight jeans, expensive leather jacket and a look that said she was clearly out of place at the 24-hour vet place on Federal. "I thought you'd come on Friday," Rachel said.

The young woman shrugged. "How's Bailey?"

"Your dog is fine. But we had to take his intestine out early Friday morning and straighten it out. We almost lost him again."

"Yuck..." she said with major distain. At that point whatever compassion Rachel had for the young woman was gone completely.

"Yeah, it's a big yuck," the older woman said, "and a big yuck means a big vet bill. We're talking $2500 at this point."

Jesse brought Bailey, who faintly wagged his tail, but the girl said nothing, but she rolled her eyes. "It's your fault," she said to the boyfriend. "You need to come up with that money."

"Hey, I don't have it. Tuition is due in a month, and there's nothing left."

"Find it. I am not going to tell my dad that I paid $2500 for that dog after you left that turkey out. He thought I was nuts to pay a thousand for it. Otherwise, we're through."

I'd take that offer if I were you. Rachel looked down at the floor.

"I don't see how a surgery for a dog could cost so much," the girl said giving the vet a mean look. "I mean, it's not like it's a person and you couldn't have been in there for hours."

No, just years of vet school and knowing that I would be operating on a dog at midnight on Thanksgiving night. Rachel wanted them out of there and wanted them out badly. "Look, the dog needs another day at least here. Come see me Monday and we'll discuss prices then."

The two left. "She drives a Hummer," Jesse said, "and then complains about a vet bill. Gas guzzling bitch."

"Don't talk that way about the clients," Rachel said. "Plus it's insulting to a dog. But if you put it on Facebook, I won't care."

"You know you could sell that dog on Craigslist if you want."

Rachel didn't respond but knelt down by the dog. "You're a good boy," she said, and he stuck his nose up against her shoulder.

They went back to see Joe after that. "How are you doing?" Jesse asked.

"Ok…I am probably getting out on Monday."

"That's great," she said. "Isn't it?"

"Umm…I don't know. I feel better than I have for a long time, but I called my sister to see if I could stay with her, and she said no. Too much old baggage."

"Do you have to stay with someone?" Rachel asked. "I mean you're not used to staying with anyone."

"No, but they think I'll do better if I have some support."

"Look, damn it!" Rachel's voice rose. "You owe me for taking of your cat. You get out; you can work it off and stay at the clinic." She walked out of the room.

"Why does she care," Joe said to Jesse. "Why do you care?"

"We're suckers for lost animals and lost souls. Maybe there's no answer." Jesse hugged the man and then followed Rachel out the door.

On Sunday Rachel went in to work because of Bailey but then stayed longer. She took the pup over to the park. The dog walked like it was an old dog but wagged its tail when she told him what a good boy he was. She flicked the switch for the second candle on the advent wreath and then cleaned the storage room.

"You're not supposed to have lit the candle," Jesse said when she came in with Joe. "It's not until next Sunday."

"What do you expect from a Jewish atheist? Besides I was lighting the candle of preparation because that's what I was doing. What are you doing here? You're early."

His hair was cut and he was shaven. "They needed my bed. So what do I do, Doc?" he asked.

"There are cages to be cleaned out," she said.

"Can I see Hope first?" He sounded like a little boy at Christmas.

She brought out the shoe box with the kitten curled in the stocking cap. "Ah, look at her," he said, looking at the squirming ball of fur.

"It is a her. How did you know?

He smiled a little smile. "I wonder if Tawnie ever got a cat," he said.

"You're not giving this cat to your daughter when you haven't seen her in a decade. That's not fair to the cat or the daughter," Rachel said. "Now if you want a Labradoodle, have I got a deal for you."

"No, probably not. Shouldn't the eyes be open?" he said as he stroked the kitten.

"Usually between a week and ten days so we're getting close.

He smiled. "That will be nice." Then he left the room, whistling a tune.

"What are we doing?" Rachel asked Jesse.

"Seeing a miracle, Doc."

The week passed. Joe had major moments of anger and despair, and Rachel stomped around like an incredibly irritated Godzilla, but Jesse kept them both going on lots of black coffee. Jesse took him to his AA meeting every evening. He slept in the storage room and fed Hope every four hours. Bailey's owner never came back, but Rachel didn't take any action against the delinquent owner. Instead she kept taking the slow moving dog out herself for a walk.

"Jesse, Doc!" Joe's voice called on Thursday when they came in one morning. "Look at Hope."

The little kitten was squirming with eyes wide open. The two women cooed together. "Look around you, kid. You're in trouble now," Jesse said to the kitten.

Joe was beaming. "She's not in trouble. She's got a good home instead of a dumpster."

"We're the ones in for trouble," Rachel said. "She's going to be running all over in a week."

They switched on the candle for joy that night. Jesse took pictures on her phone. "I'll get some prints for the office. And put Hope on Facebook."

Joe wasn't in the storage room or anywhere else in the clinic the next morning when they got there.

"What the hell?" Rachel said. "Where do you suppose he's at?

"I don't know," Jesse said. "He didn't leave a note, did he?"

"Nothing....son of a bitch," Rachel said. "I shouldn't have done this."

"What? Help him out? Why not? You don't know that he's not coming back."

"No, he'll probably come back drunk. Or maybe not at all. He's a guy. You can't trust them."

"That's not fair."

"Really? You're telling me what's fair?"

"Why are you yelling?"

"I'm not yelling." Rachel stopped herself, pinching the bridge of her nose. "I don't know why." Then she looked at the calendar. "It's the day my dad died. Maybe that's it. Someone just left again."

"Rach... it's been twelve years," Jesse said, putting her hand on her shoulder.

"Doesn't matter if it's been a hundred years. I still miss him. He would have helped Joe, and then it would have been alright. But me—I try to help and get stuck here with another cat to find a home for."

The bell to the front office door rang. "Great—more people," Rachel said.

But it was Joe. "Where have you been?" Rachel snapped.

"I went to see my sister yesterday."

"But that was yesterday. Why so slow—your cat's hungry." Rachel said.

"She didn't want to see me. I think she hoped I'd be dead." He looked down at his shoes. They were dirty.

There was silence. "Why?" Rachel finally asked.

He shrugged. "More money for her. Less to worry about once there's a funeral. She hadn't seen me sober in a long time. I guess she was more used to me drunk than sober."

"Why did you go?"

"My mom left money to give me every month. I wanted it."

"To go on a binge?" Rachel's voice was still sharp.

"No, I thought I'd give it to you, for Bailey and for Hope. It wouldn't be enough, but it's better than nothing." He reached into pocket and pulled out $200.

"It took you this long to get the money." She was still mad.

"No, after she gave it me, I sat for a long time. I went over to my ex-wife's, but they don't live there anymore. Then I went down to Civic Center Park and talked to some of the guys down there. You know, I saw guys who didn't recognize me and it's only been a week."

"Did you get drunk?" Jesse asked. Her voice was soft.

"Yeah, I did, but it didn't help. I went over to the shelter and talked to someone there. I am sorry I am so late; I didn't think you'd worry about me. But I am glad I am back." He strode back into the kennel, carrying a sack.

At lunch he came back to the front area and said to Rachel, "I brought you some latkes. There's a Jewish bakery by the shelter. The owner thought this would be something everyone would enjoy."

"I am not Jewish anymore," Rachel said, taking the bag. "Whatever, they smell good to me." She brought out latkes and sufganiyot.

"We can heat them up," Joe suggested.

"You can't heat up latkes in a microwave." For a moment Rachel remembered the smell of her mother cooking in the kitchen.

He shrugged.

"Oh, alright, we'll see." She went to the back room.

Jesse was on the computer when Rachel came in. "Is that work related?" the older woman asked.

"Nope," Jesse answered without looking at her boss.

"Then I have a ton of bills to pay that I don't need you hanging out and Facebooking your friends."

"Whatever..." and Jesse went back to metering invoices.

When they were almost ready to close, the bell rang again and Rachel called out to Jesse, "Tell them we're closed."

"No, you got to see this one. Joe, you got to help me." Jesse for once was insistent.

Rachel came out first. The young woman standing there had no animal with her. "Can I help you?" Rachel asked.

"I need to see Joe," she said, tearing up. Rachel then knew this was no ordinary customer.

"Joe," Rachel yelled, "get out here."

He came out and then stopped. "Tawnie?" he said. The girl ran and hugged him.

Rachel looked at Jesse. "Facebook?" she asked. Jesse nodded smugly. "You're going to have to show me how. How about taking a new picture of me and my dog, and we'll post it?"

Christmas Eve morning Rachel looked out the window at 7:30. There on the street stood Jesse, Tawnie and Joe, handing out cups of coffee. She went outside but didn't say anything.

"We're open tomorrow," Jesse said to a couple waiting for the bus. "In case you need a vet."

Rachel returned to the office only to find that the kitten had jumped on the counter knocking off the Advent wreath again. Rachel smiled and went back into the storage room. She found the Menorah, wiped the decade of dust off it and then slowly lit the candles. Then she picked up the wreath and placed it next to the Menorah.

Thank you for reading **A Different Kind of Christmas and Other Stories**. If you liked it, won't you please leave a review at your favorite retailer?

About Marcia Canter

Marcia grew up in South Dakota on a farm. She and her older siblings played imaginary games involving cowboys and Native Americans, riding Shetland ponies through the pastures. When left alone, she pretended to go to England by reading Black Beauty, or to Atlanta with Scarlett O'Hara, and to Alabama to fight injustice with Atticus Finch.

When she was eight years old, she start making up stories to amuse herself and others. In college she left fiction behind and majored in journalism. When she married and journalism jobs were scarce, she went into corporate business for sixteen years, eventually becoming a middle manager. She left to write the great American novel, raising her two daughters with her husband, working part time jobs, and she became active in school and church. She is currently a youth director at her Methodist Church, which she loves greatly.

But there are still stories to tell. Booklanthropy is her attempt to combine both love of books and writing, with making a bigger difference in the world via financial contributions. A portion of the proceeds from her writings will go to a cause that works to improve the world.

How to Connect with Marcia Canter

Email Marcia at marcia@booklanthropy.com

Like Booklanthropy on Facebook

Personal Blog: http://shoeontheotherfoot.wordpress.com/

Other Books Written by Marcia: **Every Woman's Tale**, a novel about a woman juggling work and family demands, and her husband's one night stand. How does one forgive someone after you've been hurt badly?

Also available is **Mosquito Madness,** a story about a fifth grade girl fighting against malaria. For more information on Marcia's books, go to Booklanthropy.com.